13 Past Midnight

by

Billy St. John

A Baker's Plays Acting Edition

Baker's Plays
7611 Sunset Blvd.
Los Angeles, CA 90046
bakersplays.com

CHARACTERS

BRENDA MOSS — 20's, a maid, bright, outgoing.

DURWOOD — 50's, a butler, very reserved, never loses his composure.

LILA LAMONT — 40's, a gossip columnist, nosey.

TONI CRAWFORD — 40's, attractive, outspoken, a soap opera star.

EVE FULTON — 30's, head soap opera writer, can be catty.

SKYLER TRENT — 40's, handsome, not too bright, a soap opera star.

KATHRYN WINSLOW — 40's, attractive, nervous, the producer's wife.

ALLISON TRENT — 40's, Skyler's wife, extremely jealous.

TALBERT WORTHINGTON — 70's, a little vague, character actor.

LOUISE BURKE — 60's, dignified, a character actress.

CHAD MARTIN — 20's, good looking, conceited, a juvenile lead.

ZARA DARE — 20's, pretty, bubbly, sexy, an ingenue.

GARY ANDERSON — 50's, stays stressed out, a tv director.

VICTOR WINSLOW — 50's, a powerful tv producer.

MAUREEN O'MALLEY — 50's, bossy, a cook.

PETE GRIFFIN — 30's, tough, a private detective.

SYNOPSIS OF SCENES

TIME: The Present.

PLACE: The game-room of Victor Winslow's mansion in Beverly Hills.

 – ACT I –

SCENE ONE: Just before midnight on a Saturday night.
SCENE TWO: 1:00 A.M. Sunday morning.
SCENE THREE: 3:00 A.M.

 – ACT II –

SCENE ONE: 4:00 A.M.
SCENE TWO: 5:00 A.M.

I would like to dedicate "13 Past Midnight" to my family:

My parents, Billy and Hazel St. John
My brother, Steve St. John
and
My sister, Connie St. John McDonald.

They are the best family anyone could ever hope
to be a part of.
It's no mystery why I love them dearly.

-- Billy St. John

13 PAST MIDNIGHT

ACT I,
SCENE ONE

(SETTING: The game room of Victor Winslow's mansion in Beverly Hills. The room is lavishly furnished. DR is a door that leads out into a small bathroom. The SR and UR walls primarily consist of built-in bookcases that contain stacks and stacks of board games such as Monopoly and Clue. A small, ornamental clock is also on the shelves, placed so that its hands are not visible to the audience. UC is a set of double doors that slide into the door frame; they are open. Beyond them we see an entry hall and the bottom steps of a staircase that continues out of sight off SR. Off UL is a door used for sound effects. A bell cord hangs SL of the doorway. Centered in the SL wall is a set of French doors that open out onto a patio. Beyond the doors is a large lawn with a stone wall in the distance. SR is a round table with four low-backed chairs around it. A Tiffany lamp hangs over it. CS is a sofa; a set of matching chairs are DL and DR of it, facing in. SL is a small table with chairs SL and SR of it; a chess board with chess pieces are set up on it. A bar spans the UL corner. On it are glasses, an ice bucket, bar towel, matches, and such. There is a bar stool behind it, and three more stools below it. A life-sized, cloth dummy, dressed in a tuxedo, sits on the chair SL of the chess table. Its hands are made from white gloves stuffed with foam rubber. A face has been painted on the stuffed cloth bag that forms its head. A dart board with darts sticking from it is on the wall DS of the French doors.)

7

(AT RISE: It is night. The room and hall LIGHTS are lit, giving the set a soft glow. Moonlight is visible beyond the French doors. The stage appears empty. After a beat, BRENDA, the maid, enters through the UC doorway from off SR, carrying a bowl of ice cubes. BRENDA is a cute, outgoing young woman in her 20's. She wears the traditional maid's black dress, white apron, and cap. She crosses to the bar. As she reaches it, DURWOOD, the butler, rises up from behind the bar, causing BRENDA to jump and cry out, startled. DURWOOD is the prototype of a butler, poker-faced, unflappable, in his 50's. He wears a tuxedo.)

BRENDA. Durwood! You nearly scared me to death!

DURWOOD. I deeply apologize, Miss Brenda, although I suppose scaring you "to death" would be most appropriate on this particular evening, would it not?

BRENDA. Huh? Oh, you mean the murder game. I'll have no part of that, thank you very much! *(Gesturing to the ice bucket on the bar.)* Would you ...

DURWOOD. My pleasure. *(He lifts the bucket lid; BRENDA pours the cubes from the bowl into the bucket; DURWOOD replaces the lid.)*

BRENDA. Thanks.

DURWOOD. You're completely welcome. I've just checked Mr. Winslow's stock of liquor beneath the bar, and everything seems in order. Does Maureen have the food prepared?

BRENDA. Almost. I've been helping her. Don't worry — we'll be ready by midnight, as ordered.

DURWOOD. *(Checking his watch.)* It's nearing twelve o'clock now.

BRENDA. (*Indicating the bowl.*) Then I'd better take this back to the kitchen and see if Maureen has any last minute instructions.

(*She exits UC and off UR. DURWOOD comes out from behind the bar and crosses to the bookcase, SR. He straightens the boxes of games on the shelves, though they are already neatly aligned. He turns toward the UC doorway when he hears voices from offstage.*)

LILA. (*Off UC.*) I think this is such fun! Leave it to Victor to come up with the idea of having a murder mystery party. Don't you love it?
TONI. (*Off UC.*) I suppose ...

(*LILA LAMONT and TONI CRAWFORD appear on the staircase beyond the UC doors. LILA is a nosey, pushy gossip columnist in her 40's. TONI is the leading lady on a soap opera. She is an attractive woman in her 40's. Both women wear evening gowns; LILA's includes a jacket with pockets. As they talk, they will descend the stairs and enter the game room.*)

TONI. (*Continuing without a break.*) ... though why he chose to make it an all night event is beyond me. All of us on the show are usually in bed by nine o'clock. If you find me sprawled out on the floor, don't assume I'm the murder victim -- I might just be taking a nap. (*They enter the room and notice DURWOOD.*) Durwood ... Are we the first? I thought Victor said at dinner we were to gather here in the game room at midnight.

DURWOOD. (*Crossing to them.*) That is correct, Miss Crawford. The others should be here shortly.

LILA. I guess we might as well find a comfortable seat, Toni.

TONI. That sounds like a good idea.

DURWOOD. Might I suggest the sofa?

TONI. You know, Durwood, after this murder is committed, you'll probably be everyone's prime suspect; you know, "the butler did it!"

DURWOOD. If you say so, madam. In the meantime, I suppose I should go off somewhere and ... "buttle." If you'll excuse me ... (*He exits UC and off SR. LILA and TONI cross to the sofa and sit.*)

LILA. (*Taking a small notebook and pen from a jacket pocket.*) I might as well begin taking notes for my column. Does the "Hold Back The Night" cast and crew socialize often off the set?

TONI. Not at all. I think we see all we want to of one another at work. We have to report to the studio by 6:00 a.m. for makeup, and are often there till 6:00 p.m., or later, just to tape one episode of the soap, and since the show runs five days a week, well ...

LILA. I can imagine. They say "familiarity breeds contempt." Come on – dish the dirt, Toni ... are there any juicy feuds I can report on in my column?

TONI. Really, Lila ... Artistic temperments flare up occasionally, but that's to be expected among creative individuals. Our little spats are not serious ...

LILA. That's not what I've heard. A little birdie told me you and Zara Dare had a knock-down, drag-out fight on the set last week. (*TONI is obviously surprised LILA knows this.*)

TONI. Zara? That little ... (*She almost uses one word, but changes to another.*) ... twit is such an amateur! She belongs in a community theatre company out in the boonies somewhere, not on America's favorite daytime drama! Why Victor hired her, I'll never know.

LILA. I can guess why — she's a very attractive young lady.

TONI. She might be attractive — in a flashy sort of way — but she's no lady! I could tell you ... (*LILA leans forward, pad and pen ready, but they are interrupted by the entrance of EVE FULTON, DR. EVE is a caustic woman in her 40's. She is dressed in a formal pajama outfit.*)

EVE. I thought I heard voices in here. Am I interrupting a private conversation?

TONI. That's okay, Eve. Come on in. (*EVE closes the door and crosses to SR of the sofa.*)

EVE. I was just using the little bathroom there. It has another entrance on the far side from the library. This mansion of Victor's is so spread out, it's easy to get lost in it. So, Miss Lamont, is Toni feeding you lots of choice tidbits for the paper?

LILA. (*Closing the pad so EVE can't see what's written in it.*) Not really; we were only chatting. (*EVE and LILA are rival writers, though they work in different media. They dislike each other and slip in barbs when they can, though they veil them with smiles.*)

EVE. I see you're ready to take notes if anything interesting occurs. I'm a big note taker, too. Sometimes in the oddest places I overhear a wonderful line I can use in one of my scripts.

LILA. I was wondering how you manage to come up with so much dialog. I really admire you creative writers who are able to turn out reams of scripts year after year after year. It's all I can do to squeeze out one little newspaper column a day.

TONI. You're too modest, Lila. You have millions of faithful fans who devour every word you write.

EVE. And what's more, they believe it. (*LILA shoots her a look. EVE flashes her a big smile.*) It's a tribute to you that your articles are so accurate ... usually. (*She starts toward the bar.*) I think I'd like a drink before this game thing gets underway. Can I get you one?

LILA. (*A little coolly.*) No, thank you.

TONI. Nothing for me, Eve.

EVE. Suit yourselves.

(*She brings out a bottle from under the bar and pours herself a drink. SKYLER TRENT and KATHRYN WINSLOW enter at the French doors, LC, and then close them. KATHRYN is an attractive woman in her 40's, beautifully gowned. Though she attempts to present a calm demeanor, an underlying nervousness shows through. SKYLER is a handsome man in his 40's, pleasant, but not too bright. He wears a tuxedo.*)

SKYLER. Hello again, all. Kathryn was showing me about the grounds. Did you know that huge stone wall runs all the way around the estate? I love the privacy.

LILA. I'm sure privacy is something you had to sacrifice, Skyler, when you became the leading man on "Hold Back The Night." It's the price of fame.

EVE. (*To LILA; slightly sarcastic.*) That's an astute observation. Did you make it up all by yourself? (*To KATHRYN, indicating her drink.*) I hope you don't mind if I've made myself at home, Kathryn.

KATHRYN. Please, do. Brenda will serve drinks later, after she's helped Maureen prepare the midnight snack.

TONI. Not more food! I'm still stuffed from dinner. I have to watch my figure; the camera adds ten pounds, you know.

KATHRYN. I know; I was an actress before I married Victor.

LILA. I remember reporting your wedding. It's a shame you gave up your career for marriage — you were on your way to becoming a major film star.

KATHRYN. Victor insisted. He said being Mrs. Victor Winslow would be a full-time job.

LILA. Any regrets?

KATHRYN. (*Unsettled by the question.*) I ... uh ...

(*She is saved from answering when ALLISON TRENT, SKYLER's wife, enters UC from off SR. ALLISON is very possessive of SKYLER, and very jealous. She wears evening clothes.*)

ALLISON. (*Hurrying over to SKYLER.*) There you are! I've been looking all over for you.

SKYLER. Kathryn showed me the grounds. It's a beautiful estate.

ALLISON. No doubt. (*To KATHRYN, a hint of suspicion showing through.*) How kind of you to give Skyler a private guided tour.

KATHRYN. Yes ... well ... if you'll excuse me, Mrs. Trent, I must check on things in the kitchen. (*She exits UC and off SR.*)

ALLISON. (*Taking SKYLER's arm.*) I need to speak with you. (*She pulls him to the UR corner of the room where they mime a conversation. She grills him about his walk with*

KATHRYN while he protests his innocence.)

TONI. (*Whispering to LILA.*) Allison is insanely jealous of Skyler. (*Noticing that LILA is jotting that down.*) Don't quote me on that!

EVE. (*Coming from behind the bar and sitting on the center bar stool.*) I'm ready to get this show on the road. Who knows? I might get an idea for a plot line from Victor's little game.

LILA. Yes ... Wouldn't it be nice if you came up with something original for the show? (*EVE lets the comment pass. LOUISE BURKE and TALBERT WORTHINGTON enter down the stairs. LOUISE, in her 60's, is the grande dame of the older soap stars, very regal. TALBERT is an elderly character actor in his 70's whose memory is not what it used to be. Both are dressed in formal clothes.*)

TONI. Louise ... Talbert... join us. (*LOUISE crosses and sits on the sofa with LILA and TONI as TALBERT sits on the chair SL of them.*)

TALBERT. Is this where we're supposed to be? Good.

TONI. I wondered where you'd disappeared to.

LOUISE. After dinner, Talbert and I slipped off to find some bedrooms and take a nap. (*To LILA.*) We were in separate rooms, Miss Lamont. Talbert and I have been man and wife so many years on the show, people seem to think we're married in real life as well.

TALBERT. It's something Edna and Tom — that's our real spouses — have got used to by now.

LOUISE. I can't imagine why Victor insisted Talbert and I take part in this mysterious game of his. He knows we're not spring chickens anymore. We need our sleep.

EVE. Before the night's over, Victor's going to make an

announcement you need to hear. (*This piques everyone's interest. The others murmur in surprise.*)

LILA. How wonderful! A scoop for my column. I don't suppose you'd give me a hint?

EVE. And incur Victor's wrath for letting the cat out of the bag early? No way.

LILA. As I said, I didn't expect you to tell me.

EVE. Since we're here for mystery games, I'll give you a clue: it will affect "Hold Back The Night."

(Now the gathering really are curious. SKYLER and ALLISON drop their topic of conversation and begin to discuss EVE's hint -- in mime. They sit at the table, SR. CHAD MARTIN and ZARA DARE enter UC from off SR. CHAD is a handsome young man who is very self-centered. He wears a tuxedo. ZARA is sexy and flirtatious. She wears a tight, flashy dinner dress. They are in their 20's.)

CHAD. See, Zara, I told you they wouldn't start without us.

TALBERT. I believe we have a few more minutes before midnight arrives, young man.

ZARA. There's Eve. (*She pulls CHAD to EVE at the bar.*) You're just the one we want to see, Eve. Chad and I have a great idea!

EVE. And what would that be, Zara? (*ZARA sits on one side of EVE on a stool, CHAD on the other.*)

ZARA. Well, since we play the youngest romantic couple on the show, we thought my character -- Lulu -- could get hit on the head and wake up expecting a baby, but she has amnesia and can't remember who the father is!

CHAD. And then Nathaniel – I – would get wildly jealous and vow to find out who got Lulu in trouble, and kill him!

LOUISE. (*Quietly, to TONI.*) I hate the idea – they'd have me knitting booties for my unborn great-grandchild till the cows come home.

TONI. (*Quietly.*) What about me? As her mother, my character would make the Guinness Book of World Records for having the longest nervous breakdown in history.

EVE. (*To ZARA.*) Have you considered this? As slow-paced as soap operas are, if we used your idea, Lulu would be pregnant for three years or so. Do you really want to wear a pillow and maternity clothes on the show for that long?

ZARA. I hadn't thought of that. It was a lousy idea. Forget it!

CHAD. (*To EVE.*) Can't you come up with something for us? Zara and I think it's time you let our characters carry the show for a while.

ALLISON. (*Quietly, to SKYLER.*) The conceited, pushy little ham! You and Toni are the stars of "Hold Back The Night" – and they were trying to turn you into grandparents!

SKYLER. What's wrong with that, Allison? You and I have a grandchild.

ALLISON. Not in public!

EVE. As it happens, we're going to introduce a new plot line on the show soon. It will affect all of the characters. That's the subject of Victor's big announcement tonight.

LILA. There you go, getting my curiosity aroused.

EVE. Don't get too curious, Lila ... curiosity kills cats, you know. (*GARY ANDERSON enters at the French doors. He is a man in his 50's who lives under stress, and has an ulcer to prove it. He wears a tuxedo.*)

GARY. You haven't begun yet -- good.

TONI. We couldn't start without our esteemed director.

EVE. The bar's open, Gary, if you'd like to wet your whistle.

GARY. I shouldn't, but my ulcer's been quiet so far, so I'll indulge. It's going to be a long night. A little fortification might be in order. (*He goes behind the bar and pours himself a drink. He will sit on the stool behind the bar.*)

LILA. Mr. Anderson, Eve has been hinting about a new development that Victor has planned for the show. Do you know what it is?

GARY. I haven't the vaguest idea, Miss Lamont, but Victor is the best producer of daytime drama in the business. I'm sure whatever he's come up with will be terrific.

SKYLER. (*Quietly, to ALLISON.*) I hope so -- our ratings have been slipping a bit lately.

ALLISON. Shuuu! (*VICTOR and KATHRYN WINSLOW enter UC from off UR. VICTOR is a powerful man in his 50's who's used to getting his way. He wears a tuxedo.*)

VICTOR. Hail! Hail! The gang's all here -- almost. Why don't you be seated, Kathryn, while I call the servants. I want everyone present when I announce the rules to my new game. (*KATHRYN sits on the chair SR of the sofa. VICTOR pulls the bell cord beside the UC doorway.*) All of you know one another, of course, but I've invited a mystery guest who should be here any minute. I asked him to arrive just before twelve o'clock. (*There is a murmur of surprised ad-libs among the others.*)

TALBERT. I must say, we are all intrigued by your actions thus far.

VICTOR. (*Crossing to CS.*) Good, Talbert -- a mystery

should be intriguing, and exciting. I promise you an evening you'll never forget.

CHAD. (*Whispering, to EVE and ZARA.*) He obviously doesn't know Talbert's memory very well.

(*DURWOOD, BRENDA and MAUREEN enter UC from off SR and stand beside the doorway. MAUREEN is a bossy woman in her 50's who doesn't take any guff from anyone. She has on a uniform appropriate for a cook.*)

DURWOOD. You rang, Mr. Winslow?

VICTOR. Yes; I want you all here for some announcements. (*The doorbell rings off SL.*) Ah, there's our last visitor. Durwood? (*DURWOOD nods and exits through the doorway and off SL. We will hear the front door open and close.*)

VICTOR. Maureen, I assume all is in readiness in the dinning room?

MAUREEN. It's as ready as it's going to be, Mr. W.

VICTOR. Fine.

ZARA. I swear, Victor, if I eat another bite, I'll just bust right out of my dress!

ALLISON. (*Muttering under her breath to SKYLER.*) If she takes a deep breath, she'll pop out of it ... and you'd better not let me catch you looking when it happens.

(*DURWOOD appears in the doorway UC with a man -- PETE GRIFFIN. PETE is a private investigator in his 30's, tough, smart. He wears a suit -- a little worn and inexpensive, but presentable.*)

VICTOR. Pete! Perfect timing — come in. (*He crosses*

toward PETE who steps down to meet him. They shake hands.)
PETE. You have a nice spread here, Mr. Winslow.
VICTOR. I like it. Durwood, if you'll activate the system?
DURWOOD. As you wish, sir. (*DURWOOD exits off SL
again. He will reappear shortly and resume his position with
BRENDA and MAUREEN.*)
BRENDA. (*Whispering to MAUREEN.*) The new guy's cute!
Wonder if he's married?
MAUREEN. (*A whisper.*) Behave yourself, girl. (*The clock
begins to strike twelve o'clock. VICTOR cocks his head to
listen, then says:*)
VICTOR. Perfect. (*Continuing over the chimes.*) I suppose
introductions are in order.
PETE. A lot of these mugs -- excuse me, faces -- already
look familiar. I been watching the soap ever since we worked
out our deal. (*The others cast curious glances at one another.*)
VICTOR. How very enterprising.
PETE. (*Not understanding the word.*) Say again?
VICTOR. It's not important. Let me tell you who everyone
is, and you can get better acquainted later. (*He will indicate
the characters as he introduces them.*) Everyone, this is Pete
Griffin. Pete's a private investigator. I've hired him to act as
a consultant on the show. Pete, over there is our leading man,
Skyler Trent, and his wife, Allison. My wife, Kathryn. These
lovely ladies are Lila Lamont, the newspaper columnist, and
two more of the show's stars, Toni Crawford and Louise
Burke. Talbert Worthington who plays Louise's husband.
Behind the bar is "Night's" director, Gary Anderson. Our
ingenue, Zara Dare; head writer, Eve Fulton; and juvenile
lead, Chad Martin. As you'll notice, they and we add up to
thirteen. That number gives us the total we need to play the

murder mystery game I'm creating. I call it "13 Past Midnight." The servants are not players; they are here to make your evening more enjoyable. Should any of you need anything, just ask ... (*Indicating them:*) ... Durwood, our butler; Brenda, our maid; or Maureen, our cook. (*The servants nod when introduced.*) Now, Mr. Griffin, if you'd like to have a seat ... (*Indicating the chess table.*) ... perhaps with our silent guest there, I'll explain what the game's all about, and why I've chosen the company present to play it. (*PETE crosses to the chess table SL and sits.*)

LOUISE. We all know how much you love games, Victor. Whatever inspired you to invent one?

VICTOR. I was going to explain that, Louise. (*He crosses to the bookcase, SR.*) As you all no doubt know, murder mystery parties have become a popular form of entertainment. Game manufacturers now produce party kits such as this one ... (*He pulls a box from the shelf and shows them the cover; it is a murder mystery game.*) ... which includes everything you need to commit a nice little murder.

ZARA. Oh, I've played one of those before. The host gives each guest a packet of cards that tells the player who his or her character is, and how the characters feel about each other — who they like, or want to kill — you know. I turned out to be the victim — everybody wanted to kill me. (*She giggles.*)

Toni. (*Under her breath to LILA.*) That host deserved an award for perfect casting.

VICTOR. Exactly. I've recently been in touch with Arthur Reeves, the president of Reeves Enterprises, a company that makes a number of such party games. I approached him with the idea of manufacturing a mystery game based on "Hold Back The Night." I've invited you here to help me develop the idea.

EVE.   And you're going to call this game "13 Past Midnight," featuring characters from the soap?

VICTOR.   That's my plan.   Actually, the game players will represent the actors who play the roles on the show, as well as some who will be staff members such as you, the head writer; Gary, the director; Lila, a gossip columnist, and so on.

SKYLER.   Who will we want to kill?

VICTOR.   Some of you will dislike one another for various reasons, and all of you will hate the producer of the show.

PETE.   Can I ask a question?

VICTOR.   Of course, Pete.   What is it?

PETE.   Why does everyone hate the producer?   When a killer bumps off somebody, he's got to have a motive — unless he's a nut case or something.

VICTOR.   Ah yes, the motive.   In our situation, one of the soap opera actors wants to kill the producer because he's going to fire him — or her.   (*There is a murmur among the others.*) Some of the crew will get the ax as well.   That is their motive for murder.

CHAD.   I'm glad it's just a game.

VICTOR.   The fact is, it's more than just a game; I really am going to make some changes on the show — drastic changes. One of the characters on "Hold Back The Night" is going to be murdered.   (*There is a surprised outburst from the others except PETE, EVE and the servants.*)

VICTOR.   Our ratings have dropped an entire point on the Neilson scale over the last few months.   Killing off a major character should revive the viewers' interest in the show very nicely.   We'll bring in a new character, a detective, who will attempt to discover the identity of the murderer.   That is why I've hired Pete, there, to serve as a consultant on the soap.

PETE. I don't mean to brag, but I've put a few bad guys in the slammer.

TALBERT. But who's getting fired? Which of us are you going to let go, Victor?

VICTOR. I'll make that announcement at 6:00 a.m. when the game ends.

KATHRYN. Victor, I think that's a terrible way to break the news to your cast. Some of them have been on "Hold Back The Night" for years.

GARY. You said crews ... ? (*At this point, VICTOR will cross to SL by the French doors.*)

VICTOR. Correct. I intend to replace some of the creative staff as well. You'll find out who in the morning.

LILA. I assume my job is to act as an investigative reporter, but one thing puzzles me — why have you included Kathryn in the game? Will her character be a suspect as well?

VICTOR. She might have the strongest motive of all, since the producer plans to divorce her — just as I've started the proceedings to divorce Kathryn. (*There is an outburst from everyone.*)

KATHRYN. (*Rising.*) Did you have to announce our divorce as part of a game!?! You are the cruelest man who ever lived!

VICTOR. We would have to tell the press sooner or later. We might as well let Lila have a scoop.

KATHRYN. You could have told her in private. Oh ... (*She turns and runs into the bathroom, DR.*)

VICTOR. See how exciting the game is already?

LOUISE. (*Chiding.*) Really, Victor ...

VICTOR. Let's proceed. (*He crosses to the bookcase.*) To simplify matters, why don't we use our own names tonight? I'll invent fictitious names for the characters later. (*He takes a poster paper sign, about 12" wide and 6" high, from a shelf. A length of string is tied to holes in the upper corners. The name "Victor" has been written on the sign in black magic marker. VICTOR carries the sign to the dummy at the chess table, SL.)* I had the prop department at the studio make me the dummy there to serve as my stand-in. Pretend he's me; I intend to circulate around the house and observe the rest of you at play. Here you go, "Victor." *(He puts the sign around the dummy's neck so that it hangs at its chest.)*

TONI. Are we supposed to ignore you if our paths cross?

VICTOR. Yes. From this point on, direct all of your hostilities toward my alter-ego here.

LILA. *(Rising.)* Victor, I'm very sorry about your problems with Kathryn, but since you were thoughtful enough to give me an exclusive, I'd like to find a phone and call it in to the paper. There's still time to make the morning edition.

VICTOR. I'm afraid that's not possible, Lila. I've switched off all the phones at a hidden control box that only I know the location of. *(LILA sits.)*

SKYLER. But why ... ?

VICTOR. It's part of the game. Also, I've had Durwood activate the computerized system that controls the lock on the main gate. An electrical current now runs through the gate as well as the wires that line the top of the walls that surround the estate. The circuitry is programmed so that the electricity will shut off and the lock disengage at 6:00 a.m. when the game concludes.

ALLISON. What if someone should become ill — or hurt?

VICTOR. I can punch in a code that shuts the program down in the advent of an emergency. I'm the only one who knows the correct numerical combination.

PETE. What if something should happen to you?

VICTOR. You would have to wait till morning to summon help. I'll take that chance. (*KATHRYN reappears at the door DR. It is obvious she's been crying.*)

VICTOR. Kathryn, my dear ... so you've decided to rejoin us. (*He crosses to her.*) I was just explaining to the others that we will be totally isolated from the rest of the world for the remainder of the evening ... trapped together ... thirteen past midnight ...

MAUREEN. (*Muttering under her breath.*) Some of the servants might be ready to kill you as well.

KATHRYN. I don't want to play your stupid game, Victor. Let me leave. I can check into the Beverly Wilshire Hotel.

VICTOR. (*Touching her chin with his finger.*) And spoil the fun? No, my darling wife — I must insist that you stay. (*She jerks away from him and crosses to the table SR where she sits with SKYLER and ALLISON.*)

VICTOR. (*Turning to face everyone.*) Before I turn you loose to play the game, there's one more thing. (*He crosses to the bookcase and takes a box from a shelf; it's similar in size to the type of box you store good silverware in. He takes it to the SR table and sets it down.*) If you're going to commit a murder, then you'll need a murder weapon, of course. I have a few handy here that you can feel free to use. (*He opens the lid.*)

LILA. But suppose we have no motive to commit a murder?

VICTOR. Then I suggest you take a weapon for self-defense. I'm sure Victor Two, over there, isn't the only potential victim in the room, though he's the most likely one. (*He holds up examples of the items he mentions, to illustrate.*) Here we have several guns; they're real, but loaded with blanks, naturally. Some of you might prefer a knife; if so, be careful — they're sharp. Bottles of poison, which is actually saccharine tablets. I've made certain the curtain ropes on the drapes in the living room are detachable should any of you wish to hang your victim.

LOUISE. You've thought of everything.

VICTOR. Oh, surely not ... Don't feel bound to stick to the weapons I've provided here. You might use a pillow from the sofa to smother your victim, or strip an electrical cord from a lamp to electrocute him or her, or maybe cosh your victim on the head with a piece of bric-a-brac from the bookshelf. Be imaginative ... be resourceful ... be creative ... Let your imaginations run wild. This is a game, after all — have fun.

CHAD. What happens after someone gets murdered? Is the game over?

EVE. Of course not; the rest of us will try to discover the identity of the killer. Right, Victor?

VICTOR. Correct. The murderer should try to get away with the crime. I can't wait to see how you all do as amateur sleuths — as well as Pete, our real detective, of course. Let the game begin! Feel free to roam about the entire house, and grounds, too, if you wish. Just be careful not to touch the gates. Also, I should warn you — I have a pair of Dobermans that normally roam the grounds at night. I've kept them in their pen tonight, naturally, but don't go near the cages. If they got free, they could hurt someone quite badly. Now — Durwood, you three are dismissed to resume your duties.

MAUREEN. And not a moment too soon, if I may say so, Mr. W. You're about to have your first corpse on your hands, 'cause my bunions are killing me.

VICTOR. (Laughing.) My apologies, Maureen.

MAUREEN. I'll overlook it this time. (To everyone.)

There's food and coffee on the sideboard in the dinning room.
Help yourselves.

*(MAUREEN, DURWOOD and BRENDA exit UC and
off SR. Everyone except KATHRYN rises and begins to
stir around. Before they leave the room, most will take
a weapon from the box. The items taken are: Guns —
LILA, TONI, SKYLER, GARY, CHAD; Knives —
KATHRYN, EVE, ALLISON, ZARA, VICTOR; Poison
— LOUISE, TALBERT. PETE will not take a weapon.
The cast ad-libs among themselves as they exit while the
following dialog ensues:)*

TALBERT. *(To LOUISE as they exit UC and off SR.)* Victor
couldn't have meant us -- surely he wouldn't give us the ax.

LOUISE. My sweet, naive Talbert ... If it would save
"Hold Back The Night," Victor would decapitate his own
mother like a Thanksgiving turkey.

ZARA. *(To CHAD, but casting her eyes at VICTOR.)* I
think I'll look around outside. Maybe I can find some
toadstools or something really neat to use as a murder weapon.

CHAD. You've got a knife.

ZARA. That's to protect myself. *(Starting toward the
French doors.)* This is fun.

CHAD. Fun? Didn't you hear what Victor said? Aren't you
worried you might be the one who gets fired?

ZARA. *(With a knowing smile.)* Oh, Victor would never fire
me. *(She pats the dummy's cheek.)* Would you? *(She calls to
VICTOR across the room.)* I'll be in the garden, Victor ...
(Suggestively.) ... if you should want me. *(To CHAD.)* See
ya.

(ZARA exits through the French doors.   CHAD turns and exits UC and up the stairs.   KATHRYN, who has remained seated at the table, observed ZARA's comment to VICTOR with a stony expression.)

LILA. *(Approaching VICTOR.)* This is so exciting! I can't wait to find out which character is going to be murdered on the show. I'll be on pins and needles till six o'clock.

VICTOR. You'll have to wait longer than that, Lila. I'm going to send you out the gate before I announce those plans. The identity of the victim will be a closely guarded secret until the day the episode airs.

LILA. But Victor ... !

VICTOR. Don't be greedy, dear heart. I've given you a number of exclusives already this evening.

LILA. *(Pouting.)* Well, if you're going to be an old meanie ... I think I'll use the loo there, and then check out the library. *(Starting DR.)* Watch your back!

VICTOR. You, too. You've written stories about some of your fellow players that were quite vicious.

(This stops LILA in her tracks for a beat, then she continues out DR. VICTOR turns, takes a knife from the box, crosses to the dummy and lays it on the table beside its hand, then exits through the French doors as KATHRYN watches. At this point KATHRYN, PETE and GARY are all who are left onstage. The characters not already specified have left at the following exits: TONI and EVE — UC and off SR; SKYLER and ALLISON — UC and up the stairs. GARY approaches PETE.)

GARY. (*Extending his hand.*) Gary Anderson; I direct "Hold Back the Night" ... unless Victor replaces me after tonight. Welcome aboard.

PETE. (*Shaking his hand.*) Pete Griffin. Thanks. It'll be neat to be involved in a murder that isn't real, for a change.

GARY. Aren't you going to get a weapon, too?

PETE. (*Patting his coat under his arm.*) No need. I pack a rod, only it ain't loaded with blanks. I can take care of myself without it, though.

GARY. I'm sure you can. Why don't we get a cup of coffee, then I can show you around the house -- mansion, really. It's quite a showplace.

PETE. Sounds good to me. Lead the way, Mr. Anderson.

(GARY and PETE exit UC and off SR. KATHRYN is left alone in the room. She rises slowly, the hard look still on her face. She stares at the dummy a beat, then grabs a knife from the box and rushes out UC and up the stairs. The LIGHTS dim to blackness, hold a beat, then rise to denote the passage of time. In the darkness, the clock strikes one.)

*

SCENE TWO

(When the LIGHTS come back up, the stage is empty. The weapons box has been replaced on the shelf. BRENDA enters UC from off SR, carrying a cup of coffee. She crosses to SL and puts it on the chess table beside the dummy. PETE enters DR.)

PETE. You sure you want to give him coffee? The caffine might be a shock to his system.

BRENDA. Oh! It's you, Mr. Griffin. Mr. Winslow told me to put a cup by the dummy in case anyone wants to poison him.

PETE. *(Crossing to her.)* I'm surprised nobody's attacked his ... what did he call it? ... stand-in, yet. The boss gave a lot of his guests some good reasons to bump him off. By the way, the name's Pete.

BRENDA. *(Offering her hand.)* Brenda.

PETE. *(Shaking her hand.)* Nice to meet you. I don't get to meet many nice girls in my line of work.

BRENDA. I don't get to meet many private investigators in mine. I've always been fascinated by men who put their lives in danger.

PETE. I've had a few close scrapes in my time.

BRENDA. I'd love to hear about them.

PETE. Maybe after this shindig is over, we can get together and discuss some cases.

BRENDA. I'd like that ... Pete.

PETE. It's a date ... Brenda.

(There is a slight noise outside the French doors. PETE and BRENDA turn to look at them. One of the doors

opens and ALLISON backs furtively into the room, looking behind her at the darkness outside. She is carrying her knife. She pulls the door shut, then turns, raising her knife high into the air, ready to stab the dummy. She freezes, startled, when she sees PETE and BRENDA there, looking at her.)

ALLISON. Oh. Hello ... *(She quickly drops her arm and holds the knife behind her back.)*

PETE. Don't mind us.

ALLISON. No, excuse me. I was just ... passing through. *(She hurries past them and exits UC and off SR.)*

PETE. That was the actor's wife, right? Trent?

BRENDA. Allison Trent, yes.

PETE. When the boss introduced me to everyone, I wondered why she was included in his game. I get the idea she's not connected to the soap opera.

BRENDA. Simple. She keeps such a tight rein on her husband, Mr. Winslow knew there was no way she'd let Mr. Trent go to an all night party without her. He had to invite her to get Skyler Trent to come.

PETE. You seem to know quite a lot about the guests.

BRENDA. Mr. Winslow talks freely in front of the servants. To him, we're no more than sticks of furniture.

PETE. I don't suppose you've overheard who he plans to knock off on the show?

BRENDA. No. As far as I know, he's kept that to himself. Pete, I'd love to talk with you some more, but I should be getting back to the kitchen and help Maureen with the dishes.

PETE. I'll walk you there. *(They start toward the archway.)* Maybe you can kind of act like my assistant? Keep your eyes and ears open for anything that might help me solve the "murder," after it happens?

BRENDA. That sounds like fun.

(They exit UC and off SR. A beat later, LOUISE descends into sight at the staircase. She looks off SR. She comes into the room, crosses to the chess table, and brings out her bottle of "poison." She pops the cap and is ready to pour some tablets into the coffee cup at the table when LILA enters DR.)

LILA. Naughty, naughty.

LOUISE. (*Startled.*) Oh! (*She quickly recaps the bottle.*)

LILA. (*Crossing into the room.*) Don't let me stop you.

LOUISE. I can hardly kill Victor in front of you, can I? The murderer is supposed to try to commit the crime undetected.

LILA. I must say, you've gotten into the spirit of the game.

LOUISE. I wouldn't be if it hadn't been for Victor's announcement.

LILA. Really? Do you think he'd really kill off your character on the show? Martha's become a soap opera institution.

LOUISE. Which is a prime reason to eliminate her — it would cause shock waves throughout the industry. What better way to gain tremendous publicity than kill of the matriarch of daytime drama?

LILA. You could be right.

LOUISE. It won't surprise me if he does away with either me or Talbert. It would mean the end of our careers if we were cut from the show. We've been identified with our characters for so many years, no one else would hire us — the other producers know audiences wouldn't accept us in any other parts.

LILA. That would be a shame. Still, I think Kathryn has the strongest motive to kill Victor ... the divorce, you know.

LOUISE. Victor has had girl friends on the side for years — usually cute little starlets, like Zara. If Kathryn knew about them and accepted his infidelities, why would he suddenly decide to cast her aside now? It'll cost him a fortune in alimony and property settlement.

LILA. No, it won't.

LOUISE. What do you mean? This is California — the community property law ...

LILA. When they became engaged, Victor insisted that Kathryn sign a pre-nuptual agreement that in the event they ever divorced, she would receive a hundred thousand dollars, period.

LOUISE. But Victor has millions!

LILA. I know. I remember thinking at the time that she was foolish to sign the agreement, but I suppose if she hadn't, Victor wouldn't have married her.

LOUISE. That scoundrel!

LILA. I agree. Kathryn could have been a major star, and become quite wealthy on her own. She deserves a lot more; Victor is getting his freedom dirt cheap. (*They hear the front door open and close off SL and turn toward the doorway, UC. TALBERT enters.*)

TALBERT. Louise ... I was wondering where you went. I took a walk outside — thought the fresh air might help me stay awake. I think I'm going to need some coffee, though. Do you remember how to get to the dinning room?

LOUISE. (*Under her breath to LILA.*) I have to look after Talbert more than I do my own husband. (*Aloud, to*

TALBERT.) It's this way, dear. I'll show you. (*She takes his arm and leads him off SR.*)

LILA. (*To herself.*) I need something stronger than coffee. (*She crosses behind the bar and kneels out of sight, looking through the bottles there.   One of the French doors opens; TONI sticks her head in and looks around.*)

TONI. (*To someone outside.*) The coast is clear. Come on.

(*She enters and opens the doors wide. LILA peeps up behind the bar, spying on the proceedings. SKYLER enters carrying a large urn in which is planted a huge bush; he strains to peer around or over it. The effect should be comical.*)

SKYLER. I'm not so sure this is a good idea.

TONI. It's a great idea. Victor said to be inventive. Well, I'll bet he never thought he'd be crushed to death by a potted plant.

SKYLER. He didn't say we could team up to kill him.

TONI. He didn't say we couldn't. This way, we can murder him together, and then give each other an alibi.

SKYLER. I'm not sure Allison would like that. She's probably looking for me right now.

TONI. Then let's hurry. You can't hit him with it here — it would damage the chess table. Wait, I'll move him. (*She takes the dummy and drags it from the chair to the DL corner where she lays it on the floor on its back.*) There. Now — drop it on the sucker.

SKYLER. I can't see ...

TONI. Here ... (*She gets behind SKYLER and guides him toward the dummy. LILA comes out from behind the bar and crosses to SR of the chess table, watching them.*) Watch out for your toes. (*This is too much for LILA. She bursts out laughing, startling TONI and SKYLER. They turn toward her.*)

LILA. I'm sorry, but the sight of you attacking Victor with a bush is just too funny. It's ingenous, but hilarious.

SKYLER. Who is it? I can't see ...

TONI. It's Lila Lamont ... (*To LILA.*) ... and you've spoiled it.

LILA. Sorry.

TONI. (*To SKYLER.*) Come on. We'll have to think of something else. (*DURWOOD enters UC and takes in the situation.*)

DURWOOD. (*His usual deadpan delivery.*) Miss Crawford ... Are you committing a murder, or did you get a sudden urge to redecorate the house?

TONI. Neither. We'll put the plant back where we found it. This way, Skyler. (*She pushes him out though the French doors. DURWOOD crosses to the doors and closes them. LILA returns to the bar.*)

DURWOOD. May I do anything for you, Miss Lamont?

LILA. No, thanks. I was about to make myself a drink when Toni and Skyler came in. (*She brings a bottle from under the bar and pours a drink.*)

DURWOOD. I assume they are responsible for placing the victim on the floor?

LILA. Yes. They didn't want to damage the table when they crushed him to death.

DURWOOD. How thoughtful – you don't often find such considerate murderers.

LILA. I'm sorry I interrupted them. I'm ready for someone to do away with Victor's double so we can start investigating the crime.

DURWOOD. There are still almost five hours left to play the game. And who knows? It might be someone else who is "done away with."

LILA. I suppose so. Well, I don't often find myself locked up for a night with several tv stars. I need to track some of them down and get some quotes for my column. I'll see you later, Durwood.

DURWOOD. No doubt, Miss Lamont.

(LILA takes her drink and exits UC and up the stairs. DURWOOD looks at the dummy, then crosses down to it. He stares at it a beat, then delivers a sharp kick to the dummy's side.)

DURWOOD. *(Softly.)* That's for you-know-what, Mr. Winslow. *(He turns and exits UC and off SR. A beat later we hear the front door open and close, and ZARA's voice.)*

ZARA. ... so then I told Chad I wasn't worried because I knew there was no way ... *(ZARA and VICTOR appear at the UC archway from off SL.)* ... you'd fire me from the show. *(She notices the dummy's empty chair at the chess table.)* Hey! Where'd you go? *(They enter the room.)*

VICTOR. *(Crossing to the dummy.)* Someone put Victor Two on the floor. There are no signs that anyone murdered him, though. Help me get him back onto the chair. *(ZARA holds the chair while VICTOR puts the dummy back at the chess table.)*

ZARA. I just love chess ... I wish I knew how to play it. You'll teach me, won't you, Victor? Once we're married and I've moved in and all ...

VICTOR. Of course, my dear.

ZARA. I think that would be good for my image — you know, smart as well as sexy. It'll be good publicity for the show.

VICTOR. But you won't be on the show.

ZARA. What!?!

VICTOR. I'll expect you to devote all your time to being Mrs. Victor Winslow. It's what I demanded of Kathryn, and she agreed.

ZARA. (*Muttering to herself.*) Yeah, and look where it got her.

VICTOR. As soon as my divorce from her is final, I'll make an appointment for you to meet with my lawyers. They'll go over the details of the pre-nuptual agreement I expect you to sign.

ZARA. Agreement?

VICTOR. Of course. It's a minor, but necessary, requirement before we take our vows. There. Now that Victor Two is back where he belongs, I suppose we should leave him alone so the game can continue.

ZARA. (*With a cold look in her eye.*) Right. The game ...

VICTOR. I have a taste for one of Maureen's delicious pastries. Join me?

ZARA. You go ahead. I need to ... check my makeup. (*Starting DR.*) I'll use the little bathroom in there.

VICTOR. Suit yourself. I'll find you when I want you. (*He exits UC and off SR. ZARA stops at the DR doorway and watches him go out. A furious expression crosses her face.*)

ZARA. (*To herself.*) Give up my career!?! Sign a pre-nuptual agreement!?! We'll see about that! (*ZARA is surprised when the DR door opens and KATHRYN enters with a laugh.*)

KATHRYN. So you're the one Victor is dumping me for. I assumed as much. I must say, his taste in women has declined over the years.

ZARA. Go ahead and insult me; I don't care. Soon you'll be out in the street and all this will be mine.

KATHRYN. But for how long? When Victor tires of you, he'll discard you for another trashy little starlet. Of course, by then, any chance you ever had for a show business career will be over -- just like mine.

ZARA. Never! I'll persuade him to let me continue acting on the show.

KATHRYN. Don't kid yourself. Victor will want you here at his beck and call. It'll be that, or nothing.

ZARA. But being a star is all I ever dreamed of! Maybe ... maybe I won't marry Victor. I might let you have him back, Kathryn. How would you like that?

KATHRYN. Victor and I are finished, regardless. If you back out, he'll find a replacement for you soon enough. (*She laughs.*) Whatever your decision, your career is over, Zara. If you refuse to marry Victor now, he'll kick you off the show for spite ... and he'll blackball you so that no one else in the industry will hire you. Victor can be very vindictive. (*She laughs.*) Face it, Zara -- either way, as an actress, you're all washed up.

(*KATHRYN begins to laugh again, and continues to laugh as she exits UC and up the stairs. With an exclamation of anger, ZARA hurries out DR. After a beat, the French doors open. TONI and SKYLER enter. SKYLER is struggling to carry a bucket of water.*)

TONI. (*Noticing that the dummy is back on the chair.*) He's not there! He's here! Victor has been moved back onto the chair.

SKYLER. I guess we should have done that. Somebody could have tripped over him on the floor.

TONI. Not everyone is as clumsy as you, Skyler.

SKYLER. Me? I'm not clumsy.

TONI. Are you forgetting the time you walked into the camera during a taping?

SKYLER. That wasn't my fault! One of my contact lenses had slipped around to the side.

TONI. I see.

SKYLER. That's more than I did.

TONI. Forget it. I can't believe we were lucky enough to find the bucket beside the spigot.

SKYLER. Toni, can we get this over with? The bucket is heavy. If I drop it, it'll splash water everywhere.

TONI. Okay! Okay! Do you want to hold that while I stick his head down in it, or vice versa?

SKYLER. It doesn't matter! Just get on with it! (*SKYLER holds the bucket DS of the chair. TONI stands behind the dummy and leans it over toward the bucket.*)

TONI. The bucket is too full! If I stick Victor's head in it, the water will run out. This is a new dress; if you make me get water on my new dress, I'll kill YOU!

SKYLER. Well, how do you expect me to get rid of it?

TONI. You can chug-a-lug it for all I care!

SKYLER. If you had let me make a noose from the curtain rope, we wouldn't be in this mess.

TONI. I told you, that's too ordinary. Any old murderer uses a noose. If we can show Victor how creative we are, maybe he won't be so quick to drop one of us from the show.

SKYLER. But if we make a puddle on his rug, he'll give both of us the boot.

TONI. You're right. This isn't going to work. Come on. (*She sets the dummy back up in the chair and starts out the French doors. SKYLER follows. TONI closes the doors behind them. EVE enters UC from off SR, nibbling a pastry, followed by GARY.*)

GARY. Come on, Eve, you can tell me.

EVE. I did tell you – I don't know who's going to be fired from the show.

GARY. Then why aren't you worried about your job? You don't seem to be in the least concerned.

EVE. Victor told me that one of the characters will be murdered. I've changed the tone of the scripts to add a mysterious air to the show – to prepare the viewers for something shocking to happen. Haven't you noticed?

GARY. Well, yes, now that you mention it.

EVE. The scripts reflect my style, Gary. Every good writer has a distinctive style. If Victor were to replace me, the style of the writing would change. No matter how subtle the differences between me and a replacement, the audience would sense the change. Now, why would Victor bring in someone new when a major plot line is developing? I think my position is safe enough.

GARY. I wasn't thinking Victor might bring in someone new, I was thinking about your assistant.

EVE. Allen? But he's ...

GARY. (*Cutting in.*) Did you notice Victor has called Allen into his office for a private conference almost every day this week?

EVE. No, I didn't. Allen didn't mention it ...

GARY. Just what could they be talking about, Eve? New scripts for the show, maybe? Imitating your style, maybe? I wouldn't be so complacent if I were you.

EVE. (*Frowning.*) I think I need to have a talk with Victor.

GARY. Good. While you're at it, see if he gives any hints about my job.

EVE. Fend for yourself. (*She starts for the DR. door. GARY starts to follow. EVE stops at the door and turns back to him.*)

EVE. Gary, please! I'm going to the bathroom. My fingers are sticky -- I'm going to wash my hands.

GARY. Sorry.

(*EVE exits DR. GARY crosses to the UC archway to exit, stops, then turns back toward the dummy. Slowly he takes his gun from his pocket and raises it, aiming at Victor Two. Before he can fire, the French doors burst open and ALLISON charges in, knife raised to stab the dummy. She halts, startled to see GARY. They hold a beat, then in unison -- and without a word -- they lower their weapons. GARY backs through the archway and off SR as ALLISON backs out the French doors, leaving them open. A beat later, we hear a clacking sound from off SR. MAUREEN appears UC from off SR pushing a carpet sweeper. She will follow the route EVE took into the game room.*)

MAUREEN. (*Muttering under her breath.*) Crumbs ... crumbs ... crumbs ... Who does the woman think she is ... Gretel?

(She comes to the spot where EVE stopped to talk to GARY and pushes the sweeper vigorously over that area several times. She raises the sweeper by the handle and starts back toward the archway. She stops, looks at the dummy, then crosses to above the chess table. She stares at the dummy a beat, then suddenly flings up her hand and pokes the dummy in the eyes with two fingers in a "Three Stooges" move.)

MAUREEN. *(To the dummy.)* You know why!

(She turns and exits UC and off SR. As she goes, TALBERT appears on the staircase and descends, then stops at the archway. He looks off SR and SL. He enters the room and crosses to the chess table. He pulls the bottle of "poison" from his pocket. He tries to unscrew the cap, but it won't come off. He performs a comical mime, trying to open the bottle, including using his teeth. It still won't open. Finally, he turns and starts out, UC.)

TALBERT. *(Forelornly.)* Louise ...

(He exits off SR. A beat later, TONI and SKYLER enter at the French doors and stop SL of the dummy. SKYLER carries a set of large hedge clippers, its blades opened wide. He holds them at the dummy's neck.)

TONI. What are you waiting for? Do it! *(SKYLER tries to snap them shut, but can't bring himself to do it. Abruptly, he hands the clippers to TONI.)*

SKYLER. I can't – it's too morbid. You do it.

TONI. I'm not strong enough to cut his head off. For goodness' sake, it's just a dummy. It's not as if it's going to spurt blood all over you. Don't be so squeemish.

SKYLER. Blood ... (*A sick expression crosses his face. He clasps a hand to his mouth and runs out the French doors as if he might throw up.*)

TONI. Oh, good grief!

(*She lowers the clippers and follows him out, disgusted. The DR door opens and ALLISON steps into the room. She has her knife raised, gripped by the blade like a professional knife thrower. CHAD enters UC from off SR and freezes when he sees her.*)

ALLISON. (*Exasperated.*) What is this place ... Grand Central Station!?! (*She storms out DR, slamming the door behind her. CHAD gets a couple of steps into the room when ALLISON flings the door open again and sticks her head into the room.*)

ALLISON. Have you seen Skyler?

CHAD. No. (*ALLISON abruptly jerks her head back out of sight and slams the door. CHAD crosses behind the bar. He puts ice into a glass and pours himself a soft drink. As he does this, he talks to the dummy.*)

CHAD. If you don't mind, Victor, I'll pour myself a soda. I've been thinking about your little announcement. (*Unnoticed by CHAD, VICTOR appears at the UC doorway from off SR. He stops and listens to CHAD's conversation with his alter-ego.*) You know what I've decided? I've decided I'm the one you're going to ax off the show. (*When he has poured his *drink, CHAD will cross to above the chess table, still unaware of the real VICTOR's presence.*) It's obvious what's going on between you and Zara. You hate it when I play love scenes with her, don't you? I noticed you came to the set last week the day we taped Nathaniel and Lulu giving way to mad passion in the Jacuzzi. You stood beside the camera and glared at me the whole time. I got so nervous I swallowed about a gallon of hot water. Well, let me tell you something, Mr. Winslow – I enjoyed the scene, in spite of you. Zara's a knockout, you know. I just think it's a shame that she had to get involved with an old fuddy-duddy like you when someone like me is available ... I mean, I've got youth, charm and good looks ...

VICTOR. And I've got brains, power and millions of dollars. (*CHAD jumps, then turns to see VICTOR in the doorway.*)

CHAD. Mr. Winslow! (*Stammering.*) I ... I ... I was just playing the game ... I didn't mean ... Sorry.

VICTOR. My arrogant young friend, you don't know what sorry is ... yet! (*VICTOR crosses out of sight SL. CHAD starts after him, stops to put his drink on the bar, then exits UC and off SL.*)

CHAD. Mr. Winslow ... wait! I didn't mean it ... Mr. Winslow ... ?

(*We hear the front door open and close twice as they leave. After a beat, LOUISE and TALBERT enter UC from off SR. TALBERT carries the bottle of "poison" in one hand, its cap in the other. They cross to above the chess table.*)

TALBERT. Thank you so much, Louise.
LOUISE. That's quite all right, dear. (*She pulls out her*

bottle of "poison.") You just have to line up the little arrow on the lid with the arrow on the neck of the bottle. See ... *(She shows him as she opens her bottle.)*

TALBERT. How very clever. If I hadn't found you, I was going to look for a hacksaw next. If we poison Victor's coffee, how will anyone know we've killed him?

LOUISE. I suppose we should leave one of the bottles beside his cup. That should do it.

TALBERT. Brilliant! *(Indicating his bottle.)* Do you want to, or shall I?

LOUISE. Why don't we both take part?

TALBERT. Wonderful idea! Ready? *(They hold their bottles over the coffee cup, but are stopped by TONI's and SKYLER's entrance at the French doors. TONI carries an ax and SKYLER carries a curtain rope with a noose fashioned at one end.)*

SKYLER. ... but how can I strangle him if you chop his head off? *(Seeing LOUISE and TALBERT.)* Oh.

TONI. *(To LOUISE, indicating the dummy.)* Have you already ... uh ... ?

LOUISE. *(Recapping her bottle.)* No. You came in before we ...

TALBERT. *(To LOUISE.)* What should we I do now?

LOUISE. Put a lid on it. *(TALBERT looks insulted.)* The poison bottle.

TALBERT. Oh. *(He recaps his bottle.)*

ZARA. *(Entering UC from off SR, her knife raised.)* Okay, Victor, you'll be sorry ... *(Seeing the others.)* Oh. *(Joining them.)* Has someone ... you know ... ?

TONI. Not yet, but the line forms to the right if you want to take a crack at him.

LOUISE. You seemed very angry just then, Zara. Has something happened we don't know about?

ZARA. Mind your own business, "Grandma"!

LOUISE. You don't have to be rude. If you really were my granddaughter, I'd send you to your room. (*GARY jumps through the DR doorway and lands in a shooting stance, his gun held before him in both hands, pointed at the dummy.*)

GARY. Prepare to die! (*Surprised to see the others.*) Uh ...

SKYLER. That was a great entrance, Gary.

GARY. (*Lowering the gun.*) It's how I had the hero enter a scene in an old movie I directed, "Attack of the Mosquito Woman."

ZARA. I don't think I ever heard of it.

GARY. It never got released – it really sucked. (*Crossing to the others.*) Am I too late? I mean, has somebody already ... ?

THE OTHERS. (*In unison.*) No.

(*ALLISON runs in DR, her knife raised, screaming a continuous "Aiiiii ... !" Halfway in, she sees the others; without hesitating a step or lowering her knife or missing a note, she swerves US and her cry turns into a disappointed "Awwww ..." as she runs out the archway UC and off UL. We hear the front door open and slam shut, cutting off her wail. The effect is rather like a demented banshee has put in an appearance. At this point the cast is grouped in a semi-circle around the chess table thusly: <SR to SL> GARY, ZARA, LOUISE, TALBERT, TONI, SKYLER. There is a stunned silence for a beat, then TONI says to SKYLER:*)

TONI. I'll bet you have a really interesting home life. (*The French doors burst open, making everyone jump, as ALLISON charges in, stopping beside SKYLER.*)

ALLISON. It WAS you I saw! Where have you been!?!

SKYLER. Uh … Toni and I decided to kill Victor together.

ALLISON. (*Suspicious.*) You and Toni, huh? What's the matter, you don't see enough of each other at the studio? If you're going to do something fun like commit a murder, it's only right that you do it with your wife.

SKYLER. Yes, dear. (*Simultaneously, EVE enters DR with her knife as KATHRYN enters UC from off SR with hers, speaking at the same time.*)

EVE. Okay, Victor, you want to play …

KATHRYN. I'm really going to enjoy this …

EVE & KATHRYN. (*Seeing the others; in unison.*) Oh.

TONI. A couple more men and we can form a glee club.

EVE & KATHRYN. (*Indicating the dummy; in unison.*) Has anyone … ?

THE OTHERS. (*In unison.*) No. (*EVE and KATHRYN cross to the game table SR and sit, dejected. The front door opens and closes. CHAD is heard off SL.*)

CHAD. So you won't listen to me, huh? Well, I'll show you … (*CHAD enters UC with his gun drawn and stops when he sees the others.*)

LOUISE. (*To TONI.*) There's your tenor.

CHAD. I don't understand …

TONI. You seldom do.

CHAD. (*Indicating the dummy.*) Has … ?

THE OTHERS. (*Cutting in; in unison.*) No.

CHAD. Oh.

*(He sits at the game table SR with EVE and KATHRYN.
LILA appears at the stairs. She descends and crosses to
the archway, UC, singing to herself.)*

LILA. "When a body meet a body, coming through the
rye ..." (*She cranes her head to look at the dummy. She opens
her mouth to say "Has anyone killed Victor?", but before she
can get the first syllable out, everyone else says:*)
THE OTHERS. (*In unison.*) No.
LILA. It is rather difficult to tell. I wish you'd get on with
it so I can join the game.
PETE. (*Entering DR.*) What's everybody in here for? You
all look like you're at a wake -- but you can't have a wake until
you have a body.
SKYLER. We've tried to do away with Victor ...
TONI. (*Cutting in.*) LORD KNOWS we've tried ...
SKYLER. ... but we keep getting interrupted.
ALLISON. I've been on freeways that had less traffic.
PETE. (*Thinking.*) Ummmm ... I've got an idea. Miss
Lamont, would you mind giving that cord a jerk -- the one that
calls the servants?
LILA. Certainly. (*She pulls the cord.*)
KATHRYN. Speaking of jerks, has anyone see Victor? The
real one.
CHAD. He was outside a few minutes ago. Why? Did you
want to see him?
KATHRYN. (*Holding up her knife.*) While I've got this, it's
probably better if I don't. (*DURWOOD appears at the UC
doorway from off SR.*)
DURWOOD. There was a bell; am I supposed to guess who
rang it?

PETE. I called for you, Durwood. Would everyone else clear out, please? But don't go too far.

EVE. Can I ask what you're going to do, Mr. Griffin?

PETE. I'm going to make it easier for one of you to commit a murder. (*Everyone but PETE and DURWOOD ad-libs that that's a great idea as they leave through various exits. Finally, only PETE and DURWOOD are left.*)

DURWOOD. Is there a problem, sir?

PETE. (*Crossing to him.*) Yes, but we're going to fix it. There are too many players attempting to knock off Victor, there, and they keep stumbling all over each other. One way to commit a crime and get away with it is to do it in the dark. I guess you'd know where the circuit breakers for this part of the house are?

DURWOOD. All circuit breakers are located in the pantry, sir.

PETE. Good. Then let's pave the way for a murder. (*They exit UC and off SR. After a beat, we hear the front door open and close. VICTOR appears at the doorway, UC. He looks around, then crosses to above the chess table. He picks up the knife he laid on the table earlier.*)

VICTOR. I'll take this if you don't mind, Victor Two. I could need it more than you do. I have a feeling I might have pushed some of our players too far.

(*He crosses to the door DR and exits. The stage is still for a beat, then the room and hall LIGHTS go out, plunging the stage into darkness except for faint moonlight at the French doors. All happening close together, there are gun shots fired from the DR doorway, the staircase, the SR and SL edges of the UC*) *doorway. Figures enter the French doors and UC archway and cross to the dummy. Voices mutter in the darkness, comments such as "That's my foot," "Oh, excuse me," "Watch where you're going," etc. The cast clears off and the LIGHTS come back on. Victor Two has been thoroughly attacked: there are two knives protruding from his chest and three from his back; the rope noose is around his neck; a plastic bag is over his head; two "poison" bottles lie on the chess table beside the coffee cup which is overturned. We hear BRENDA's voice from off SR.)*

BRENDA.   Your plan must have worked — there were gunshots. *(She and PETE appear at the archway from off SR. They look at the dummy.)* Oh, boy, did your plan work!

PETE. It might be easier to find out who DIDN'T kill him.

BRENDA. And you want me to be the one who finds the body?

PETE. You're the perfect choice since you're not one of the suspects. I doubt if the killer — killerS — will come back until the victim is discovered.

BRENDA. Now?

PETE. Now.

(BRENDA lets out a blood-curdling scream. Cast members appear at the following entrances: TONI, SKYLER, ALLISON — French doors; TALBERT, LOUISE — DR; KATHRYN, LILA — the stairs; GARY, EVE — off SR; CHAD, ZARA — rise up from behind the bar.)

SKYLER. Now what do we do?

TONI. We're suppose to act -- ACT!

SKYLER. (*Pointing at the dummy.*) Look! Victor has been stabbed!

GARY. Shot!

EVE. Hanged!

ZARA. Smothered!

LOUISE. Poisoned!

TALBERT. (*Slightly overlapping LOUISE, softly.*) Poisoned.

CHAD. Do you think he's dead? (*The others look at CHAD as if to say, "You dolt!" and say in unison:*)

THE OTHERS. He's dead!

CHAD. Just asking!

ALLISON. What should we do with the body?

PETE. If I could put my two cents in ... ?

KATHRYN. Of course, Mr. Griffin — you're the expert.

PETE. I think we should cover it with a sheet or something and put it where everyone can get to it to look for clues.

KATHRYN. An excellent suggestion. Brenda, would you please bring a sheet from the linnen closet?

BRENDA. Oh sure, Mrs. Winslow. (*BRENDA exits UC and up the stairs.*)

GARY. Where do you want to put him?

PETE. How about there in the corner? That's out of the way.

GARY. Chad, help me. (*GARY and CHAD take the dummy and set him on the floor, DL, so that it's seated and leaning against the wall, under the dart board. BRENDA returns with a white sheet and gives it to PETE.*)

BRENDA. Here you are.

PETE. Thanks, dollface. (*He and GARY drape the sheet*

over the "body" so that it's completely covered.)

VICTOR. (*Entering DR; applauding.*) Bravo! Someone finally figured out how to set the scene correctly for a murder to be committed. If I had to guess, I'd bet it was you, Pete.

PETE. You got it, boss.

VICTOR. Thank you. I'll have to be sure to include a blackout in the game instructions when they're published. Just out of curiosity, how was I killed?

SKYLER. You were stabbed ...

GARY. ... shot ...

EVE. ... hanged ...

ZARA. ... smothered ...

LOUISE. ... and poisoned.

TALBERT. (*Slightly overlapping LOUISE, softly.*) Poisoned.

VICTOR. Fabulous!

SKYLER. How are we going to find the murderer? I mean ...

VICTOR. (*Cutting in.*) I know what you mean -- there are more murderers than innocent bystanders. We'll have to pick just one deadly attack and assume it's the one that killed me. You say I was smothered?

ZARA. Somebody put a plastic bag over your head.

VICTOR. How clever of them! If I have to go, I prefer to be murdered in style. How do you suggest everyone proceed in discovering who smothered me, Pete?

PETE. The first step would be to question the suspects, then we could start looking for clues.

VICTOR. Ah -- questions! I'll call this section of the game "The Third Degree"! All right, everyone, you heard Pete. Why don't you pair off in different rooms and question one another about your motives, alibis, and such. Then you can change partners until everybody has questioned everybody else. I'll wander in and out among you and take notes.

PETE. If I can throw out a suggestion? Assume each person you're grilling is guilty – listen close to all the testimonies and see if any suspect slips up. Lots of thugs get caught because they can't keep their stories straight.

VICTOR. Good advice! Well, what are you waiting for? Go play detective! Have fun! Enjoy the game! (*Everyone except PETE and VICTOR leaves through various exits, ad-libbing quietly among themselves.*)

PETE. You seem to be pleased with the way things are going, boss.

VICTOR. Oh, I am, I am. One thing I haven't done yet is get a look at the "corpse." (*He crosses to DL, kneels, and pulls the sheet down to the dummy's waist.*)

PETE. (*As VICTOR makes his examination.*) This reminds me of that Agatha Christie story – what's it called? – where the detective – Hercules (*He uses the American pronunciation.*) something – discovers that all the suspects took turns stabbing the victim. All of them could be charged with attempted murder, I guess, but since there was no way to tell which blow killed the dead guy, none of them could be prosecuted for the actual murder.

VICTOR. So you're a fan of mystery novels ... so am I.

PETE. I saw the movie.

VICTOR. (*Looking at the dummy.*) The characters in that story couldn't have done a more thorough job than my guests did. (*He recovers the dummy.*) Obviously they are playing "13 Past Midnight" with great enthusiasm.

PETE. There's no doubt about that. I guess I should join the others and start grilling suspects, too.

VICTOR. (*Crossing to him.*) Any ideas who did it?

PETE. Not yet. I noticed someone removed the knife that was lying on the chess table earlier, so I assume one of the suspects who stabbed him took it to replace the weapon they used, but we're looking for the killer who put a plastic bag over the victim's head, so that's a useless clue.

VICTOR. You're very observant. I'll be surprised if you don't turn out to be the winner of my little puzzle.

PETE. I won't if I don't get busy. 'Scuse me ... (*He exits DR. VICTOR pulls the missing knife from a pocket.*)

VICTOR. (*To himself.*) The knife wasn't taken to provide an alibi, Mr. Griffin — it's for self-defense. (*The LIGHTS lower to denote the passage of time. In the darkness, the clock strikes 3:00.*)

*

SCENE THREE

(The LIGHTS come back up on an empty room. After a beat, MAUREEN enters UC from off SR, carrying a dish towel. She crosses to the chess table and shakes her head at the overturned coffee cup. She leans over to sop up the coffee when VICTOR enters through the French doors, leaving them open.)

VICTOR. Maureen ... What are you doing?

MAUREEN. I thought I'd clean up the spilled coffee, Mr. W. Since you let the housekeeper and the other maids except Brenda off for the night, I figured I'd help keep things straight.

VICTOR. That's fine, except leave this room as it is. I don't want you to disturb any clues the players might come across. *(Unnoticed by MAUREEN or VICTOR, the DR door opens part way; an unseen observer eavesdrops on them.)*

MAUREEN. If that's the way you want it.

VICTOR. You don't like me very much, do you, Maureen?

MAUREEN. I don't like you at all, Mr. W.

VICTOR. *(Laughing.)* That's too bad, because I like you. You're one of the few people I know who will always give me an honest answer. Why do you dislike me so?

MAUREEN. Because of what you're doing to Miss Kathryn. In the years we've worked for you, Durwood and I have come to like her a lot. We think your "swapping her in for a newer model" really stinks.

VICTOR. *(Not so amused anymore.)* Watch what you say, Maureen.

MAUREEN. If you don't want to know what's on my mind, don't ask me. I'm not afraid of you, Mr. W. What's the worse thing you could do to me? Fire me? I'm a good cook and I can get another job just like that. (*She snaps her fingers.*)

VICTOR. (*Annoyed.*) I suggest you attend to the one you have now. There have been people in and out of the living room; why don't you see if it needs tidying up?

MAUREEN. You're the boss. (*She starts out UC.*)

VICTOR. Maureen ... (*She turns back and looks at him questioningly.*) Don't tell anyone I'm in the game room. I plan to hide behind the bar and see if any of the players discover any clues in here. (*The DR door closes softly.*)

MAUREEN. Like spilled coffee that's going to ruin a perfectly good table ... but it's your table.

VICTOR. Precisely. (*MAUREEN exits UC and off SR. A light breeze flutters the curtains at the French doors. VICTOR crosses to them and looks out.*)

VICTOR. Ah, good ... (*He crosses to above the dummy and talks to it.*) It's clouding over. Maybe we'll get a storm; that would provide the perfect atmosphere for our party. (*Suddenly the stage goes dark. This time there is no moonlight to reveal what's happening. Someone moves into the room.*)

VICTOR. Who is it? Who's there? (*There is no answer.*) You're really into the game, whoever you are. (*He chuckles.*) Ah, I know who it is. You're the only one who wears that very distinctive brand of cologne. What's the matter – did you leave a piece of incriminating evidence behind? Pray continue – I'll stay out of your ... (*Instead of the word "way," VICTOR emits a strangled gasp. There is a choking sound, then the sound of something heavy hitting the floor. Someone moves about in the darkness. After a few moments. we hear BRENDA's voice from off SR as she moves to the UC archway.*)

BRENDA. Pete? Are you in there? Why didn't you warn me you were going to create another blackout? Pete? (*No one answers.*) Matches ... There should be some matches on the bar. (*She moves to above the bar.*) Here they are ...

(*She strikes a match. She is standing behind the bar at its SR end. The dummy appears to be standing right beside her to her left, held in place by someone who is stooped out of sight behind the dummy. BRENDA screams. She flings back her arms in fright, causing the match to go out. She stumbles blindly to above the sofa.*)

Help! Oh please, somebody help me! (*We hear PETE's voice UC.*)
PETE. Brenda? Is that you? Where are you?
BRENDA. Over here behind the sofa. Oh, Pete ...
PETE. (*Feeling his way to her.*) I'm here. You're safe.
BRENDA. It was awful! Hold me, please hold me!
PETE. No problem. Tell Pete what happened.
BRENDA. I came in after the lights went out. I thought you might have been here. I found some matches on the bar and when I struck one, the dummy was standing right beside me.
PETE. Standing?
BRENDA. It was STANDING! The knives were still in its chest, and the noose around its neck, and the bag over its head. It looked horrible!
PETE. Stay here. I'll have a look. (*He crosses to the bar.*)
BRENDA. Pete..!
PETE. Don't worry. (*PETE strikes a match at the bar. He looks behind it.*) There's nothing here.

BRENDA. It was there! I swear that thing was there! (*The room and hall LIGHTS come back on. Apparently, the dummy has been put back under the sheet in the DL corner where it sits propped up against the wall.*)

PETE. I believe you, but whoever was taking him for a stroll obviously put him back where he belongs. (*BRENDA crosses to PETE, UL. He puts an arm around her.*)

BRENDA. If that was somebody's idea of a joke, I don't think it was very funny. It nearly scared the life out of me, and I'm not even playing Mr. Winslow's dumb game. (*LILA enters DR, her pad and pen in hand.*)

LILA. I heard a scream -- has anyone been hurt?

BRENDA. No, Miss Lamont, I screamed because I was frightened.

LILA. That's a good reason. (*She crosses to the SR sofa chair and sits as we hear the front door open and close. SKYLER and ALLISON appear in the UC archway from off SL.*)

SKYLER. What's going on?

ALLISON. We were in the garden when we saw all of the house lights go out.

PETE. I figure it was one of the boss's pranks.

ALLISON. That sounds like him. Let's take a break, Skyler. (*They cross to the sofa and sit as KATHRYN comes down the stairs and to the archway.*)

KATHRYN. Where is Victor? This plunging the house into darkness has got to stop! Someone could get hurt.

LILA. You're right, and I plan to sit right here until we're sure the lights are on for good.

KATHRYN. I'll join you. (*She crosses to the SL sofa chair and sits as LOUISE and TALBERT appear UC from off SR.*)

LOUISE. Why did the lights go out again?

TALBERT. I thought I had suddenly died.

LOUISE. Then we heard a scream.

TALBERT. That's when I knew I was still alive.

BRENDA. I'm the one who screamed. I'm sorry.

LOUISE. Come, Talbert, you need to sit down. (*She leads him to the table SR and they sit as GARY leaps through the DR doorway, gun in hand, into a shooting stance.*)

GARY. Freeze, suckers! I heard a scream -- has there been another murder?

PETE. Not that we know of. You can relax, Mr. Anderson.

GARY. Oh ... well... (*He joins TALBERT and LOUISE at the SR table as ZARA enters through the French doors.*)

ZARA. What's happened now? I was looking for clues outside when I heard a scream.

LILA. It was a false alarm; everyone's fine.

ZARA. You know, I'm getting a little tired of this game. I could have broken a heel running to the house. I'll bet I got grass stains on my shoes as it is. (*She sits SL of the chess table, removes a shoe and inspects it as DURWOOD and MAUREEN enter UC from off SR. DURWOOD stops SL of the archway; MAUREEN continues to BRENDA.*)

MAUREEN. That was you that screamed, wasn't it? Did you hurt yourself in the dark?

BRENDA. I'm all right -- I just got a scare.

MAUREEN. Mr. W's game is getting too dangerous. I was taking a fresh pot of coffee off the stove when the lights went out. I could have been burned.

KATHRYN. You weren't hurt, were you, Maureen?

MAUREEN. Don't you fret yourself about that, Miss Kathryn. Lucky for me, I know that kitchen so well I can move about in it if I was blind – which I was, for the moment.

PETE. (*Crossing up to DURWOOD.*) Did you turn the lights out, Durwood? On Mr. Winslow's orders?

DURWOOD. Not I, sir. Whoever switched off the circuit breakers not only darkened this wing, they shut off the current to the entire house. Luckily, I was able to find a flashlight and turn the breakers back on again. (*TONI and EVE appear on the stairs. They descend and enter the game room.*)

EVE. (*Angry.*) Just wait till I get my hands on him!

TONI. You and everyone else, I imagine. (*At the archway.*) We heard a scream.

LOUISE. Brenda got a scare.

TONI. Who didn't? Let's join the party, Eve. (*They cross to the bar and sit on two DS bar stools.*)

LILA. We've kept hearing about Brenda's scare — what frightened you, dear?

BRENDA. I was coming into the game room when the lights went out. I could sense there was someone in here with me. I remembered there were matches on the bar, so I felt my way to it and struck one. Mr. Winslow's dummy was standing right beside me. I screamed and the match went out.

GARY. It was STANDING beside you!?!

PETE. It had to be held up by someone crouching behind the bar.

KATHRYN. I'll bet it was Victor — that's the kind of cruel joke he'd pull.

ZARA. (*Looking at the sheeted body DL.*) Well, ol' Victor Two seems to have got back under the covers. (*Everyone turns to the French doors as they hear CHAD's voice from off SL.*)

CHAD. Ouch! Son-of-a-gun! I'd better move you before someone else falls over you and breaks his neck. (*CHAD appears at the French doors holding the dummy.*) I don't know which of you tossed the dummy outside, but it was a dumb thing to do. I fell over it and nearly cracked my kneecap. (*Everyone stares at him, then slowly they turn their heads in unison to look at the sheeted figure DL.*)

CHAD. What? What is it?

ALLISON. If Chad found that outside ...

SKYLER. Then what's under the sheet ... ?

(*As if on cue, a spot of bright red blood appears on the sheet at chest level. It spreads and begins to grow quickly until the stain is very large. Everyone seems to be shocked. Some gasp. ZARA stiffles a cry with her hand. The seated characters rise; those SR move to their left to get a better look. PETE moves slowly to DL and kneels US of the sheeted figure. He takes pulls the sheet down off the figure's head to his chest. It is VICTOR. He is dead, a shocked expression frozen on his face. A dart from the board above his head has been driven into his neck to its feathered hilt. Blood has run from the wound down his neck to his chest where it began to seep through the sheet. Everyone reacts; KATHRYN screams, then wheels away, facing SR. She grips the back of the chair with one hand and brings her other hand to her throat.*)

KATHRYN. Victor ... is he ... ?

PETE. He's dead. Someone has stabbed him in the neck with a dart. They got him in the jugular vein. He's been bleeding for quite a while – the blood has just now run down to his chest. (*He pulls the sheet back up over VICTOR's head.*)

LILA. But ... but since we're all locked inside here, that means ...

PETE. Yeah ... that means the murderer is one of us. (*The LIGHTS dim out as the curtain closes.*)

*

INTERMISSION

*

ACT II,
SCENE ONE

(A half hour or so has passed. VICTOR's body is gone, as are CHAD, GARY and DURWOOD. The dummy has been placed on the chair SL of the chess table. The knives, bag and noose have been removed from it. The remaining cast members are seated thusly: ALLISON, EVE, SKYLER – SR table; MAUREEN, KATHRYN, LOUISE – sofa; LILA – SR sofa chair; TALBERT – SL sofa chair; BRENDA – SL bar stool; ZARA – center bar stool; TONI – chair SR of chess table. PETE is pacing DR. He stops when the clock strikes 4:00 as everyone listens silently to the chimes. Faint lightning and dim thunder can be seen and heard occasionally through the French doors; they will grow in intensity as the act progresses.)

LOUISE. Two more hours ... Surely there's something we can do -- some way we can contact the police ...

PETE. Not unless we're able to find Mr. Winslow's hidden cut-off switch to the phones. You have no idea where it is, Mrs. Winslow?

KATHRYN. None. Last Wednesday Victor gave all the servants the afternoon off and insisted I go visit my sister. He had the house entirely to himself. When I arrived back here late that afternoon, a truck from the telephone company was just leaving. Victor told me he had had them install his hidden switch for tonight's game.

SKYLER. I know! We can call the phone company and ask them where ... (*His voice trails off as he realizes what he's saying.*) ... oh.

ZARA. (*Under her breath to BRENDA.*) It's a cinch Skyler didn't stab Victor with the dart — he'd never figure out you could use it as a weapon.

LILA. Couldn't we search for the device?

PETE. I guess we could, but if it's hidden in a house this big, we'd be lucky to find it before the gates open at six. (*DURWOOD, CHAD and GARY appear at the stairs. They descend and enter the room. PETE crosses to them.*)

DURWOOD. We did as you requested, Mr. Griffin. Mr. Winslow's body is in his bedroom. It is locked. Here is the key. (*He hands PETE a key.*)

SKYLER. I would have helped carry the body, but I have this thing about ... you know ... that sticky red liquid.

TONI. We know, Skyler. You get sick at the sight of tomato juice.

ALLISON. That proves Skyler couldn't have killed Victor.

EVE. Are you forgetting Victor was stabbed in the dark? I'm sure Skyler could have murdered him as long as he didn't have to see the ...

SKYLER. (*Cutting in.*) Don't say the word!

EVE. Sticky red liquid.

GARY. (*Crossing behind the bar.*) If nobody objects, I think I'll make myself a drink.

PETE. Wait, Mr. Anderson. Don't touch anything. The killer was behind the bar at one point, when Brenda almost caught him removing the dummy. He might have left some evidence behind.

TONI. He or she — the dummy's not that heavy; I moved it myself earlier tonight when Skyler and I were trying to kill him — I mean "it."

PETE. Good point. Actually, I think it would be a good

idea if we sealed off this room until the cops have a chance to inspect it. (*To KATHRYN.*) Can that be done?

KATHRYN. Only if someone remains in here. The far bathroom door, the French doors, and the sliding doors can all be locked from inside, but their locks are built in — they don't have keys.

PETE. That'll work. I'll have Brenda lock herself in here.

MAUREEN. Brenda? Why her? I don't want the girl put in danger if the killer has a reason to want to return to this room.

BRENDA. Don't worry about me, Maureen. I'll be fine.

PETE. I'll come back and stay with her after I take a look around outside. I want to see if I can figure a way to short-circuit the current that's running through the gate.

GARY. This might sound chauvinistic, but wouldn't you rather have a man guard the place? I could stay.

PETE. I'm afraid not, Mr. Anderson. Brenda is the only one of you I feel certain didn't kill Mr. Winslow. She nearly walked in on the murderer while he — or she — was committing the act.

ZARA. We only have her word for that.

BRENDA. It's true!

PETE. You all saw how pale and frightened she was. I believe her. (*Most of the others ad-lib they agree.*)

KATHRYN. (*Rising.*) If that's settled, I plan to lie down for a while in my room — with THAT door locked. (*The others rise.*)

CHAD. (*To PETE.*) Do you think the rest of us are in any danger, Mr. Griffin?

PETE. I wouldn't think so — unless any of you know something about the murderer that the killer doesn't want to be revealed. (*The others ad-lib softly that they don't know anything about it. Everyone except BRENDA and PETE starts out UC with the exception of LOUISE who starts DR.)*

LOUISE. I think I'll find a book to read in the library.

PETE. I'll secure the bathroom door behind you.

TALBERT. *(To LOUISE.)* Maybe I can find something to read, too — anything but a murder mystery. *(LOUISE, TALBERT and PETE exit DR.)*

LILA. *(Whispering to BRENDA.)* I'm probably the only other one besides you who had no reason to kill Victor. There's something I need to check in here. I'll come back after the others have cleared away.

BRENDA. But ... *(LILA leaves UC. PETE enters DR. He and BRENDA are alone.)*

PETE. I took care of that door. How do the sliding doors work? *(They cross to the UC doorway. BRENDA slides the doors closed from within the door frame.)*

BRENDA. The lock is here — you just push this button. *(She locks them.)* Do you have to go outside? It's going to storm any minute.

PETE. I really do need to see if there's a way to get out. We've got to get the cops here as soon as possible. *(They cross to the French doors.)*

BRENDA. Then please be careful. It's as black as pitch out there.

PETE. I can take care of myself. If anyone tries to get in, pull the bell cord. That should summon help.

BRENDA. Pete ...

PETE. There's no time. Lock the doors behind me. Keep this for me till I get back.

(He takes her into his arms and kisses her. He exits

through the French doors. BRENDA smiles to herself, then quickly shoots the bolts at the top of the doors into their matching holes in the upper door frame. She pulls the sheers closed across the doors. Lightning flashes in the distance, followed by thunder. BRENDA shivers and moves away from the doors to UC. She casts a wary glance at the dummy. There is a soft knock at the UC doors, startling her.)

LILA. (*Off UC.*) It's me -- Lila. Open the doors. (*BRENDA turns to the UC doors, hesitates, then unlocks them. LILA slides the doors open, slips inside, then closes them.*)

BRENDA. I'm not supposed to let anyone in.

LILA. Shoot, I didn't kill Victor. I need to find out who did, though. If I can catch his murderer, it would be the scoop of my career.

BRENDA. How do you hope to do that?

LILA. By finding clues, my dear. I've already discovered one.

BRENDA. You have? What?

LILA. Look over here. (*LILA crosses to DL. BRENDA follows. One of the doors UC slides open a crack. Someone beyond them eavesdrops on BRENDA and LILA.*)

LILA. Did you notice when the men moved Victor, a knife fell from his hand? Like the ones he gave out for the game?

BRENDA. I didn't see that; I looked away.

LILA. The detective picked it up and slipped it into his pocket, but I saw him. After the body was removed, I came over here and looked down at the floor. (*She stoops.*) That's when I discovered this. (*BRENDA stoops beside her.*)

BRENDA. It looks like a scratch.

LILA. It is a scratch; I'm sure Victor made it with the knife before he died. I believe he was trying to tell us who murdered him.

BRENDA. How could he know who it was if it was dark?

LILA. I don't know – perhaps they said something, or maybe he touched the killer and recognized them that way. I'm sure he scratched this mark onto the floor as a dying clue.

BRENDA. But what is it? It's not really a letter – an initial. It looks like an upside down "V."

LILA. That or a circumflex.

BRENDA. A what?

LILA. A circumflex looks like an inverted "V." It's a diacritical mark used over certain vowels in some foreign languages. Most newspaper columnists have symbols like that on our typewriters.

BRENDA. Would Mr. Winslow be familiar with it? If he was, what was he trying to tell us? (*LILA and BRENDA rise.*)

LILA. That's what I have to figure out. I suppose he could have been trying to carve an "M," but died before he could finish it. "M ... " That could stand for "Maureen," the cook, or Chad "Martin," or ... I've heard Kathryn mention your last name, dear – now what was it ... ?

BRENDA. Moss.

LILA. (*Moving cautiously away from BRENDA.*) Okay ...

BRENDA. Miss Lamont! You said yourself I had no reason to murder Mr. Winslow.

LILA. Well ... none that I know of. You're an attractive young woman. Victor could have tried to force his attentions on you

BRENDA. He didn't! I don't know about Mr. Martin, but I'm sure Maureen didn't kill him either. I mean, why would she?

LILA. You can't deny that Maureen is devoted to Kathryn. She might have done away with him for her mistress' sake.

BRENDA. I don't understand ...

LILA. If Victor had divorced Kathryn, she would have got a pittance of his fortune. As his widow, she'll be fabulously wealthy.

BRENDA. Still, I don't think ...

LILA. (*Cutting in.*) Never underestimate anyone's ability to commit a murder. I've been in the newspaper business long enough to know the atrocities we humans are capable of — even the most seemingly innocent among us.

BRENDA. You've become a cynic, Miss Lamont.

LILA. I've become a realist, my dear. If you'll excuse me, I'm going to the library and see if I can find any other meaning for the symbol Victor scratched in the floor. Victor was a game player — if he knew he had but moments to live, he might have tried to name his killer by using a code. I intend to be the one who deciphers it.

BRENDA. Good luck. If you want to go through the bathroom to the library, I'll lock the door behind you.

LILA. Thank you.

(*They exit DR. The doors UC close quietly. A beat later, BRENDA enters DR. She looks at the UC doors, then rushes to them to lock them; when she gets there, they slide open revealing DURWOOD. BRENDA gasps.*)

DURWOOD. (*Slipping into the room and closing the doors behind him.*) It is only I, Miss Brenda. I came to make sure you're all right. Why weren't these doors locked?

BRENDA. They were, but ... never mind. I was just about to lock them again.

DURWOOD. Miss Brenda, there's something I wanted to ask you ... privately.

BRENDA. What's that?

DURWOOD. When the lights went out – the second time – were you in the kitchen before you came in here?

BRENDA. No, I was in the hallway. Why?

DURWOOD. I was hoping you'd be able to corroborate Maureen's alibi when we're questioned by the authorities. By the time I found the flashlight and passed through the kitchen to get to the circuit breakers, she was gone.

BRENDA. Surely you don't believe ...

DURWOOD. (*Cutting in.*) Of course not. But what you and I believe, and what the police believe might not be the same.

BRENDA. It appears that most of the people in the house were alone when the lights went out. I wouldn't worry about Maureen being suspected any more than the rest of us.

DURWOOD. Perhaps you're right. I'll check on her in the kitchen. The doors ... ?

BRENDA. Yes.

(*He slips back out, closing the doors behind him. BRENDA locks them. There is a flash of lightning beyond the French doors, followed by thunder. In the distance, off SL, we hear a muted cry and the barking of dogs. The sounds grow louder as they come closer. BRENDA rushes to the French doors and pulls the sheers aside enough to peer out. Above the barking of the dogs, we hear PETE cry out:*)

PETE. (*Off SL.*) Brenda! Open the doors! Quick!

(*BRENDA frantically unbolts the doors. PETE flings them open, runs in, then slams them shut. The wild barking and snarls are now just outside the doors. The doors slam inward as the dogs apparently fling their bodies against them. PETE presses his back to the doors to keep them from breaking, but the impact nearly knocks him down.*)

BRENDA. What ... !?!

PETE. The Dobermans! Someone turned them loose! Pull the bell cord ... hurry! (*BRENDA runs to the cord and pulls it, then unlocks the UC doors and slides them open.*)

BRENDA. Durwood! Help! (*The barking reaches its peak as the doors seem ready to splinter. DURWOOD rushes into sight UC from off SR.*)

DURWOOD. Whatever has happened!?!

BRENDA. Someone opened the dog cages! (*DURWOOD rushes out of sight, SL. We hear the front door open and close.*)

DURWOOD. (*Off SL.*) Edgar! Agatha! Come! (*The crashing stops at the doors. The barking sound moves away.*) Silence! (*The barking stops.*) Come with me.

BRENDA. (*Rushing to PETE.*) Pete! Are you okay?

PETE. I'll let you know when I check the seat of my pants. If those monsters didn't get a chunk out of me, it's not because they didn't try. I think someone just attempted to kill me — or at the very least, put me out of commission.

BRENDA. Come over here and tell me what happened. (*He leans on her, winded, as she leads him to the sofa. They sit.*)

PETE. I was nearly to the gates when someone bashed me in the back of the head with rock.

BRENDA. Oh, no ... Did you see who it was?

PETE. No idea. They hid behind a tree and came up on me from behind. I went out like a light. I must have been unconscious for several minutes. When I came to, the Dobermans were rounding the corner of the house and coming right at me.

BRENDA. Why would anyone want to set them loose?

PETE. To stop me from finding a way out. I figure the killer has a reason to want to keep us trapped on the estate for another couple of hours. That would give them time to destroy any evidence ...

BRENDA. (*Cutting in.*) Evidence! In the excitement, I nearly forgot. Lila Lamont was in here. She found a mark scratched into the floor ...

PETE. I was wondering if anyone else noticed that. I figured Mr. Winslow made it.

BRENDA. So did she. She said it could be some kind of punctuation mark. She's in the library now, trying to find if it has some other meaning. (*DURWOOD enters UC from off SR. He comes to SL of the sofa.*)

DURWOOD. Mr. Griffin ... Are you all right, sir? I assume the dogs were trying to attack you.

PETE. You got that right, Durwood. They didn't get me, but a two - legged dog did. Somebody cracked me in the head with a rock.

DURWOOD. Oh, dear ... Can I get you anything? Iodine? A wet towel?

PETE. It didn't break the skin. I'll be okay. Tell me, Durwood, who could have released the dogs without being attacked by them themselves?

DURWOOD. Any of the guests who are familiar with the household — and most of them have been here before. There's a button by the side door that leads to the cages which opens them electronically. During inclement weather, especially, we can release Edgar and Agatha without going outside.

PETE. And who can control them? Who have they been trained to obey?

DURWOOD. Mr. and Mrs. Winslow and myself.

PETE. I see. Well, thanks, Durwood. I owe you one.

DURWOOD. My pleasure, sir. If that's all ...

PETE. Yeah.

BRENDA. Thanks from me, too, Durwood.

DURWOOD. You're most welcome, Miss Brenda. (*He exits UC and off SR.*)

PETE. I have a feeling it's more important than ever to keep this room guarded.

BRENDA. You think the murderer might try to scratch out the mark on the floor?

PETE. If they think no one has seen it yet. There could be other evidence they need to destroy as well. To do that, they have to go through me. (*He pats his coat over his gun.*) That reminds me ... (*He reaches inside his coat and pulls out his gun.*) It's my rod — I wanted to make sure whoever hit me didn't pull a switcheroo with one of the blank pistols. (*He replaces the gun in its holster.*)

BRENDA. What should we do now?

PETE. (*Rising.*) We might as well take a look around the room and see if we can find ... (*He is interrupted by the sound of a cry from off SR. BRENDA rises.*)

BRENDA. Miss Lamont ... ! (*PETE hurries out DR, though

*still a little shaky. BRENDA waits anxiously. PETE reappears
after a beat.)*
    PETE. The library lights are out! I can't find a switch!
    BRENDA. It's by the door that leads to the hallway.
    PETE. Matches!

*(BRENDA runs to the bar and gets a pack of matches.
She carries them back to PETE. Before she can give
them to him, LILA staggers to the DR doorway. A
stream of blood runs from her hairline, down the side of
her face. She is dazed, unable to speak. She is
clutching a book. She raises it and holds it out toward
PETE, a beseeching look on her face, as she staggers
a couple of steps toward him. She stops, drops the
book, sways, then starts to crumple. PETE catches her,
picks her up, and places her on the DR sofa chair. She
lies very still. PETE feels her pulse.)*

    PETE. She's dead. *(BRENDA emits a soft cry. PETE parts
LILA's hair and looks at her scalp.)* Somebody hit her with a
hard object ... it cracked her skull. *(BRENDA picks up the
book and steps down to PETE.)*
    BRENDA. Poor woman. She was trying to give you this.
    PETE. *(Taking it from her.)* "The House of Seven Gables"
by Nathaniel Hawthorne. "Nathaniel ..." That name rings a
bell. Where have I heard that name recently?
    BRENDA. I don't know any Nathaniels.
    PETE. It'll come to me. This book must be a clue to the
killer's identity. Miss Lamont used her last ounce of strength
to get it to us. I'll take a look in the library and see if I can
find anything else.

BRENDA. Do you have to?
PETE. I'll be safe. Whoever murdered Miss Lamont will be long gone by now. The matches?

(BRENDA gives him the matches she's been clutching. He gives her the book and exits DR. BRENDA lays the book on the SR table. She crosses to the bell cord and pulls it. PETE enters DR carrying a heavy plaster bookend; there is a spot of blood on it. He has his handkerchief across his hand to protect any fingerprints on the weapon. BRENDA crosses to him.)

PETE. I found the light switch. This was on the floor. It has to be the murder weapon.
BRENDA. Maybe the killer's fingerprints are on it.
PETE. Hopefully. We'll make sure no one touches it until the cops have a chance to inspect it. (*He puts it on the SR table next to the book. DURWOOD appears UC from off SR. He sees LILA.*)
DURWOOD. Miss Lamont ...
BRENDA. She's dead, I'm afraid. The murderer has struck again.
PETE. Durwood, can you summon everyone and have them come here?
DURWOOD. Immediately. (*He slides the doors shut.*)
BRENDA. It seems like this night will never end. (*PETE takes her into his arms in an embrace.*)
PETE. It will end.
BRENDA. As horrible as it's been, it still has one bright spot — it's the night I met you.
PETE. Yeah. I'm grateful for that, too. (*TONI enters DR.*)

TONI. Oooops! Sorry. I didn't mean to interrupt anything. The bathroom door was open. (*PETE and BRENDA step apart.*)

PETE. That's okay. Durwood is sending all the others here.

TONI. Really? Have you solved the crime? Do you know who murdered Victor?

PETE. Not yet, but whoever it is has also murdered Miss Lamont.

TONI. (*Shocked.*) Lila ... ! (*BRENDA gestures to the SR sofa chair. TONI crosses to below the sofa and looks down at LILA. She gasps and brings a hand to her mouth. She sinks down onto the sofa.*)

TONI. Why ... ?

PETE. We think she discovered the identity of the killer. (*The UC doors slide open. KATHRYN is there.*)

KATHRYN. Durwood said Lila ... (*Her voice trails off as she sees the body. She crosses to the sofa and sits beside TONI.*)

KATHRYN. It's true.

PETE. 'Fraid so. (*CHAD and ZARA descend the stairs and enter.*)

CHAD. (*To PETE.*) You sent for us? (*ZARA notices LILA and gasps. She clutches CHAD's arm. He follows her stare and reacts surprised.*) Miss Lamont ...

BRENDA. She's dead. (*ZARA and CHAD cross to the bar stools and sit. LOUISE and TALBERT appear on the stairs. They descend and enter.*)

LOUISE. Durwood said Lila has been murdered ... (*She sees LILA.*)

PETE. I'm sorry to tell you that she has, Miss Burke.

LOUISE. Pushy, headstrong Lila. Don't get me wrong – I liked her ... but she should have stuck to her gossip column and left the crime scene to someone else. *(She sits on the sofa. TALBERT looks bewildered. He crosses to the SL sofa chair and sits.)*

TALBERT. Sad ... sad ... *(SKYLER and ALLISON appear on the stairs, descend, and enter the room. They react to the body. SKYLER looks ill.)*

ALLISON. It's happened again.

SKYLER. I can't look ...

(ALLISON leads him to the bar. She seats him on the stool behind the bar, wets a bar towel in the ice bucket, and places it on his forehead. He holds it in place as she crosses below the bar and sits on the vacant bar stool there. GARY and EVE enter UC from off SR.)

GARY. Mr. Griffin, I ...   *(He stops when he sees LILA. DURWOOD and MAUREEN enter UC from off SR. MAUREEN gasps.)*

DURWOOD. I see everyone is now aware of the latest development.

MAUREEN. Someone hit her ...

PETE. Miss Lamont is no longer with us. Durwood, Mr. Anderson, would you be good enough to carry her body to one of the upstairs bedrooms?

GARY. Of course. *(EVE crosses to the chair SR of the chess table and sits. DURWOOD lifts LILA under her arms as GARY lifts her under her knees. They carry her to the UC archway. PETE follows them. MAUREEN turns her head away.)*

BRENDA. Maureen ... Here, sit down. *(BRENDA leads her to the table SR where they sit. DURWOOD and GARY carry*

LILA through the doorway. PETE closes the sliding doors as he says to BRENDA.)

PETE. Make sure no one touches the bookend.

TONI. Is it the murder weapon?

PETE. Apparently. The cops will want to dust it for prints.

TONI. Lila could be a real pain in the neck sometimes, but why would anyone want to kill her?

PETE. (*Crossing to the SR table.*) We think -- Brenda and me -- that she discovered who bumped off the boss. That person realized she knew, and hit her with the bookend. Before Miss Lamont died, she managed to stagger in here with a book ... (*He picks it up.*) ...this book, which she was determined to give to someone. We believe it's a clue to the identity of the killer.

KATHRYN. What book is it? (*PETE turns the book towards her; on the jacket cover is a picture of the house of seven gables, the title, and the author's name.*)

PETE. "The House of Seven Gables" by Nathaniel Hawthrone.

EVERYONE. (*Except Chad, Pete, Brenda & Maureen.*) Nathaniel!?! (*They turn their heads to stare at CHAD.*)

CHAD. Hey! Don't look at me!

ZARA. But that's the name of the character you play on the soap!

PETE. That's it! That's where I heard the name!

CHAD. (*Rising.*) So what!?! It's a coincidence! She couldn't have meant me!

PETE. (*To everyone.*) I guess it's okay to tell you now -- the boss left a clue to the identity of the murderer as well. Earlier tonight he apparently took the knife he had put beside the dummy there. As he lay bleeding to death, he managed to carve a mark on the floor. Looking at it from his perspective, it forms an upside down "V."

BRENDA. If he was trying to make an initial, he could have carved half an "M" before he died.

EVE. "M" as in "Martin"!

CHAD. (*Moving in front of the French doors.*) No! I'm innocent! You can't prove I killed anyone!

(*The UC doors slide open as DURWOOD and GARY enter. As attention is diverted to them, CHAD slips through the sheers, opens the French doors, and runs out. Lightning flashes near by, followed by thunder. Wind billows the sheers into the room. ALLISON rushes to the doors and shuts them.*)

GARY. What was that?

SKYLER. Mr. Griffin thinks Chad is the murderer. Chad got hysterical and ran out.

DURWOOD. He cannot leave the estate for more than an hour.

PETE. I'll find him.

ZARA. (*Rising.*) I don't think Chad did it, in spite of your clues. He's just not the type who could kill anyone.

PETE. Hopefully the cops will be able to tell if he's guilty or not. The book and the scratch on the floor are circumstantial evidence, but if Mr. Martin's prints are on the bookend, that would be concrete evidence that would nail him.

EVE. What now? Do we sit here and wait till six o'clock when one of us can go for the police?

ALLISON. Do you have any better suggestions, Eve? (*PETE stares down at the book jacket, seemingly lost in thought, as the dialog continues.*)

MAUREEN. I do. Mr. W. instructed me to prepare breakfast for five o'clock. That's what I was doing. It's almost ready, if anyone would like to eat.

TALBERT. Food?

TONI. I'm not very hungry.

PETE. (*Snapping out his trance.*) It wouldn't be a bad idea if everyone ate something. Once the cops get here, it will take them hours to question you and examine the bodies. You'll all need your strength.

TALBERT. I wouldn't mind some Wheaties ...

MAUREEN. I'll put the food on the dining table. Whoever wants it can help themselves.

PETE. Thanks, Maureen. Durwood, can you help in the kitchen? I want Brenda to lock herself in here with the bookend till I find Mr. Martin.

DURWOOD. As you wish. (*Everyone who is seated rises. They all ad-lib about getting some food, and start UC and off SR. BRENDA comes down to PETE. DURWOOD exits DR.*)

BRENDA. You think Mr. Martin might try to come back in and destroy the bookend?

PETE. If I was the killer, I'd try to get rid of it -- or wipe it clean. There's no certainty there are legible prints on the weapon, but I wouldn't take that chance if it was me. If the murderer does come back, I want to make sure you're safe. I have a plan ... (*He leans in and whispers to her. A surprised look comes over her face. DURWOOD enters DR, crosses to the French doors, and locks them. The others have left the room.*)

DURWOOD. All but the hallway doors are secured, Mr. Griffin.

PETE. Thanks, Durwood. (*DURWOOD nods, exits UC and off SR.*)

BRENDA. That's amazing! How did you think of it?

PETE. I'll tell you later. Don't let anyone in till I get back.

BRENDA. I won't.

(*They cross to the UC archway. PETE steps through it and slides the doors closed behind him. BRENDA locks the doors. She turns back into the room. There is a flash of lightning beyond the French doors. A FIGURE is silhouetted there. BRENDA gasps. The thunderclouds release their rain; it pounds down on the patio outside the doors. BRENDA rushes to them and pulls the sheers aside to look out.*)

BRENDA. (*Quietly, to herself.*) Mr. Martin ... ? (*There is a soft knock on the UC doors. BRENDA crosses back to them.*)

BRENDA. Who is it?

KATHRYN. (*Off UC.*) Kathryn Winslow.

BRENDA. Just a moment. (*She unlocks the doors and slides them open part way for KATHRYN to enter.*) Is anything wrong, Mrs. Winslow?

KATHRYN. No, it's nothing like that. I needed to see you alone. I plan to speak to each of the household staff privately. I just want to let you know how much I appreciate the support you've given me during the last few months. I'm sure you've all felt the tension that was building between Victor and me. It wasn't always pleasant around here. Once the estate is settled, I plan to raise your salaries and discuss other benefits I want to provide you.

BRENDA. That's very sweet of you, Mrs. Winslow. You've

always been very nice to us, very fair. I'm glad things turned out so that you'll have the house, and all. Not that I meant Mr. Winslow any harm!

KATHRYN. (*Squeezing her shoulder.*) I know what you meant. Thank you, Brenda.

BRENDA. You're welcome, Mrs. Winslow.

KATHRYN. I'll see that everyone is getting served. Chad ... I can't believe it was Chad.

BRENDA. I wouldn't have thought he would have the nerve to kill anyone, either -- much less two people.

KATHRYN. Yes ... well ... (*She slips out the UC doors and closes them. BRENDA locks them, turns forward, and says softly to herself:*)

BRENDA. If Pete is right, we'll be in for some even bigger surprises before the night is over. (*Thunder and lightning. The LIGHTS fade out to denote the passage of time. In the darkness, the clock strikes 5:00.*)

*

SCENE TWO

(The LIGHTS fade back up on BRENDA lying on the sofa, apparently asleep. The storm continues. Lightning flashes at the French doors revealing, once again, A FIGURE in silhouette beyond the sheers. THE FIGURE knocks loudly on the doors. It is EVE.)

EVE. Brenda! It's Eve Fulton! Let me in! *(BRENDA opens her eyes, sits up, and looks at the French doors.)* Hurry! Unlock the doors! *(BRENDA rises and rushes to the French doors. She unbolts them. EVE steps in. She wears a wet raincoat with a hood.)*

BRENDA. Miss Fulton ...

EVE. *(Cutting in.)* It's the detective — he's been hurt!

BRENDA. Pete!?!

EVE. I decided to search for Chad myself. I thought if I could find him, I could talk him into giving himself up. I didn't find him, but I found Mr. Griffin. He's lying by the tool shed, unconscious. *(She takes off the raincoat and hands it to BRENDA.)* Here — put this on and see if you can revive him. I'll try to get a first aid kit.

BRENDA. *(Putting on the coat.)* He's alive ... ?

EVE. I think so. If you talk to him, maybe he'll respond to you.

BRENDA. I hope you're right! Get some of the men to come carry him inside!

EVE. I will, just hurry! *(BRENDA exits into the storm. EVE crosses above the sofa to the table SR. She stares at the bookend a beat, then picks it up and throws it to the floor, smashing it. [Or wipes it frantically with the handerchief.]*

BRENDA steps through the French door, back into the room.)

BRENDA. You haven't ruined the real murder weapon, Miss Fulton -- the one with your fingerprints on it. It's hidden safely away. That one was its mate; we dipped it in the blood Miss Lamont shed on the library floor.

EVE. (*Cold.*) We?

BRENDA. Pete and I. He figured out the clues your victims left didn't point to Mr. Martin, but to you.

EVE. (*Crossing to above the sofa.*) Then I'll have to eliminate him as well. I had planned to take care of you away from the house -- at the tool shed -- after I dealt with the bookend. Chad could have taken the blame for that murder too. Tell me, how did your friend, the detective, come to discover I had killed Victor and Lila?

BRENDA. The realization struck him when someone called you by name as he was looking at the illustration on the book cover: Eve -- gables. Pete knew in a flash that Mr. Winslow had carved the eave of a house. Miss Lamont realized that, too, when she saw those seven gables on the jacket. You must have been in the library with her at the time. What happened? Did her expression give her away?

EVE. Yes. I could tell the moment she put two and two together. You should have seen the fear in her eyes when it dawned on her she was talking to a murderer. We've disliked each other for years. It was a pleasure to smash her skull with a bookend. When she screamed, she managed to knock it from my hand and turn out the light switch. I had to escape before I could finish the job and wipe my prints off the weapon. (*Crossing to BRENDA.*) I have to destroy it, of course. Everyone will think Chad did it. He'll take the rap for all the murders -- Victor, Lila, Mr. Griffin -- and you.

BRENDA. (*Turning and crossing SL of the chess table to below it.*) Why? Why did you kill Mr. Winslow in the first place?

EVE. (*Crossing SR of the chess table to below it, next to BRENDA.*) Gary told me earlier tonight that Victor had been meeting secretly with my assistant. He suggested Victor might be planning to give me the ax. I got him alone later and insisted he tell me if it was true. He admitted it. He said it was time to pump fresh blood into the writing. I was going to be fired. The character he planned to do away with was Lulu – Zara. Victor was going to make her give up her career when he dumped Kathryn and married her.

BRENDA. Miss Fulton, hasn't this gone far enough? Why don't you give yourself up and ...

EVE. (*Cutting in.*) Never! Not while there's a chance to save my career. When the new producer takes over the soap, he'll depend on us "old timers" to carry the show. I'll do what I have to do to keep my job. (*She pulls a gun from her pocket.*) Now give me the bookend.

BRENDA. You can't threaten me with that; it's one of the guns Mr. Winslow gave out – it's loaded with blanks.

EVE. It was before I exchanged them with the bullets I took from the detective's gun after I knocked him out. Luckily, the guns are the same calibre; I learned all about firearms when I had to research them for a murder on "Hold Back The Night" years ago. I'll ask you one more time – where is the bookend?

BRENDA. I won't tell you.

EVE. I think you will. (*With her free hand, she grabs BRENDA's throat and pushes her against the DL wall. She points the gun in her face.*) I can make your death quick and easy, or I can make it painful. Tell me -- where is the book end!?!

(BRENDA emits a pained gasp.   Suddenly, the "dummy" comes to life. It leaps to its feet, grabs EVE's shoulder, and spins her around to face him, releasing BRENDA. EVE cries out in fright. The dummy grasps her wrist, forcing her gun hand at the floor. The gun goes off, firing a harmless shot. The dummy twists her wrist, making her drop the gun. With her free hand, EVE grabs the cloth at the top of the dummy's head and pulls off the hood. Revealed beneath it is PETE.)

EVE. You! You tricked me!

PETE. It's the only way I could think of to force you to admit your guilt. If you didn't leave a legible set of prints on the bookend, I couldn't prove my hunch. If the evidence pointed to both you and Mr. Martin, the law couldn't prosecute either of you for murder. You would have got away with it. *(EVE jerks loose from PETE and crosses DC, rubbing her wrist.)*

EVE. So you devised this trap to catch me. Very clever. You should have become a writer, Mr. Griffin. Television could use your talents.

BRENDA. The law can use them better — when he puts criminals like you behind bars.

PETE. *(To EVE.)* You're pretty clever yourself. I'm glad you told Brenda about switching the blanks and bullets. I thought of someone swapping guns, but not them. If I'd made my move sooner, I would have found myself eating lead. *(He picks the gun up off the floor.)* I think you'd better have a seat over there.

*(He motions toward the SR sofa chair. EVE goes to it
and sits. There is a pounding at the UC doors, and
voices ad-libbing comments such as "What
happened!?!", "I heard a shot!", "Open the doors!",
and such. BRENDA crosses to the UC doors and
unlocks them. EVERYONE EXCEPT CHAD rushes in.
They spread US. MAUREEN grasps BRENDA's hands
in hers.)*

MAUREEN. Brenda! Have you been hurt!?! Are you all
right!?!

BRENDA. I'm fine, Maureen. The danger's over. Pete
caught our murderer. It's Eve Fulton. *(There is a shocked
outburst from the others.)*

KATHRYN. *(To EVE.)* You killed Victor? Why?

EVE. He deserved to die!

PETE. Mr. Winslow was going to fire her. His murder lead
to another, and almost two more.

BRENDA. *(Returning to PETE, DL.)* But you stopped her.
I'm so proud of you!

PETE. *(Putting an arm around her.)* It's all in a night's
work, sweetheart. *(CHAD enters through the French doors.
He is sopping wet. He crosses to above the chess table.)*

CHAD. I'm back. I've been thinking about it, and I've
decided to let the police arrest me. Let them take me to trial —
they can't prove I murdered anybody. By the time I'm found
"not guilty," the publicity will have made me an international
star! *(He turns to PETE with his arms outstretched, wrists
together for the cuffs.)* Put the cuffs on me!

TONI. Chad ... you're all wet!

(The OTHERS except EVE begin to chuckle at CHAD's confused expression. The sound grows to full-fledged laughter as the LIGHTS fade and the curtain closes.)

* * *

PROPS

PRE-SET ON STAGE AT RISE

At Bar: Liquor bottles, soft drinks, glasses, ice bucket, matches, towel.

In Bookshelves: Games, clock, box of weapons, "Victor" sign.

PERSONAL PROPS

ACT I

Bowl of ice cubes -- Brenda
Watch -- Durwood
Notebook and pen -- Lila
Cup of coffee -- Brenda
Potted plant -- Skyler
Bucket of water -- Skyler
Pastry -- Eve
Carpet sweeper -- Maureen
Hedge clippers -- Skyler
Ax -- Toni
Noose -- Skyler
Sheet -- Brenda
Dish towel -- Maureen
Dart hilt, blood -- Victor
Gun -- Pete

ACT II

Book: "The House of Seven Gables" -- Lila
Bookend, handkerchief -- Pete
Gun with blanks -- Eve

PRODUCTION NOTES

STORM

A scoop light can provide the lightning, a tin sheet the thunder, and the wind can be made by a fan or by waving a sheet of stiff cardboard offstage. The rain sound effect can be taped.

VICTOR'S MURDER

When the lights go out, Victor can slip offstage through the French doors and apply the dart hilt and blood to his neck. During this time, a stagehand can take the dummy behind the bar to scare Brenda. When her match goes out, Victor can take the dummy's place on the floor. In his upstage hand, he can hold a turkey baster filled with stage blood, his thumb covering the open end, across his chest. A stagehand covers him with the sheet. On his cue to bleed, Victor can move his thumb and squeeze the blood from the turkey baster onto the underside of the sheet. When Pete moves the sheet to lower it, Victor can slip his hand and turkey baster to his side so that his body hides it from the audience. During this blackout, you'll avoid using lightning flashes so that Victor's and the stagehand's exits and entrances won't be seen.

DOBERMAN ATTACK

The Doberman attack on Pete can be an exciting scene in the show. Simply tape the sound effect of dogs barking and make the dogs seem to come closer by bringing the recorder nearer the French doors as you increase the volume. A stagehand dressed in black will actually crash against the doors – the black night outside and the sheers across the doors will prevent the audience from seeing the cause of the blows. The lightning mustn't flash during this scene, of course.

www.ingramcontent.com/pod-product-compliance
Lightning Source LLC
Chambersburg PA
CBHW070638120726
47909CB00004B/1488